THE SEVENTH STAR

by Marjory Hall

All the girls in Portsmouth are in a flurry over the handsome, moody, naval captain. It is the autumn of 1777. John Paul Jones is waiting for his ship to be completed in the New Hampshire shipyards . . . and he is staying in Priscilla's house. Surely she is the luckiest girl in the world!

Someone from almost every family in town will sail with the *Ranger,* so everyone feels involved in her launching and her future. Gathering in secret to make a flag as a gift for the captain, Priscilla and her friends work carefully with whatever materials they can gather together in the scarcity of wartime. Stitching the seventh star in the circle, Priscilla dreams that the captain will see it—her particular star—and think of her.

As it turns out, it is young Mark Jaffrey who watches the flag through four years of sea action. Priscilla's dreams—made up of a red ball gown, a blue cloak, and a white wedding dress—sail with the ship, but they don't divert Priscilla from the action on shore. She tangles with a Tory spy and manages to get into quite a lot of trouble before she decides which man she is waiting for.

This story is Marjory Hall's seventh about an American legend. Like the others it is an exciting interweaving of fact and fiction, with a heroine who will appeal to girls who are very much *today.*

THE
SEVENTH
STAR

Westminster Press Books
by Marjorie Hall

See the Red Sky
A Hatful of Gold
Drumbeat on the Shore
The Treasure Tree
Another Kind of Courage
The Gold-lined Box
The Seventh Star

THE
SEVENTH
STAR

by Marjory Hall

THE WESTMINSTER PRESS
Philadelphia

Published by The Westminster Press ®
Philadelphia, Pennsylvania

PRINTED IN THE UNITED STATES OF AMERICA

*For Priscilla of
Odiorne's Point*

Contents

Chapter 1

THE CAPTAIN

IF I CAN reach the white gate before that cart does, he will be at home when I get there," she muttered to herself. The farmer's cart, bumping slowly along the rutted surface of Pleasant Street, was a great deal nearer the Governor's mansion than she was, but Priscilla gathered her skirts in her hands and began to run. Ever since she could remember, she had played this little game. By pitting herself against a moving carriage, the pace of another person on the street, or guessing which lamp would be lighted first, she foretold, or pretended to foretell, future events.

As the second oldest of the seven Purcell sisters, Priscilla knew she should long ago have outgrown such childish nonsense. To be sure, for a while she had outgrown it. But things had changed. Everything, she thought as she reached the gate in a flurry of whirling skirts just before the rumbling cart, everything had changed in this year of 1777. Her life. Portsmouth. The Province of New Hampshire. The whole thirteen colonies, perhaps! And all because of one person.

Breathing quickly, Priscilla slowed her steps to a more ladylike gait and walked demurely along Pleasant Street.

The shadows were beginning to lengthen and deepen, and a sudden chill wind ruffled her chestnut hair. A sea turn, she thought with the wisdom of a girl born and brought up on the seacoast. She pulled her cloak around her and hurried on.

"If Mr. Woodbury Langdon's carriage turns toward The Parade, he will be at home when I get there," she breathed to herself, her eyes fastened on the shining carriage with its glossy black horses. "Oh, *please* let it turn to the left when it reaches the corner!" She was so intent on the direction the blacks would take that she stumbled over a root and almost fell, but she jerked herself erect with an impatient exclamation. "It turned!" she crowed inwardly. "He will be there when I get home."

"He," of course, was The Captain. The Captain had been, indeed, the subject of conversation all afternoon, while Priscilla and Dorothy Hall had strolled along as close to the waterfront as they could, choosing the roundabout way in the vain hope of seeing him. They had walked from Stoodley's Tavern to the mill at the mouth of South Mill Pond, and they had never ceased to talk of the glamorous and handsome Captain John Paul Jones.

The presence of the Captain in Portsmouth was a source of never-ending pleasure to the people of the town, especially to the ladies. Young and old, they had fallen under the spell of the young officer from the moment he had arrived. July 12, 1777—it would be engraved forever on their minds. Slight, not tall, Captain Paul Jones had black hair and glowing dark eyes that pierced deep into those of any lady with the courage to gaze into his. His skin was darkened by his years at sea, so that he had, the ladies claimed, a Latin look to him, as though he had come to their world from Italy, or Spain. It always came as a surprise to hear someone murmur, "He was born in Scotland, you know. He says he is more Scottish than was Captain MacPhaedris himself!" And then they tittered. There was such a difference between the elegant young captain and the dour husband of Priscilla's great-aunt Sarah whose eccentricities lived on in local legend.

In addition to his dark and romantic good looks, the Captain spoke French and Spanish—"perfectly, perfectly," the women sighed. Somehow this accomplishment added immeasurably to his charm. If anything else was needed to make the Captain thoroughly attractive, there were tantalizing hints about his past.

"His name," they whispered, "is not really Jones. He was born John Paul. Paul the last name, that is. It is said that as late as four years ago there was no Jones attached to his name at all."

"He has been in trouble somewhere," the whispers went on. "Not his own fault, of course. You can tell that to look at him. But deep trouble. Perhaps that is why he changed his name."

"I heard he took over a ship once as was skippered by a J. Jones, and since he must sign the papers with that name he just kept it."

"No," it was asserted, "there was something to do with his acquiring his brother's estate in Virginia. The brother had been adopted by a Jones, and it was a condition for the Captain's taking on the property at the brother's death. He—"

But it was much more exciting to believe that the handsome young man was fleeing from some early trouble in his life. There could be any number of startling and romantic reasons for adding a Jones to one's name!

Oh, the Captain was perfect. And not only the women

found themselves captive to his charm. The men liked him too, that was plain. Before he had been in Portsmouth more than two or three weeks, he was one of them, one of the well-to-do patrician group that made up Portsmouth's society.

"And he lives in your house!" Dorothy exclaimed frequently to Priscilla. "Imagine! In your house. He sleeps under the same roof. And he eats at your table."

"Yes, but I don't," Priscilla retorted frequently. "Eat, I mean, at our table."

"But you see him. You even serve him sometimes," Dorothy reminded her.

"So do you, when he sups at your uncle's tavern."

"It's not Uncle Elijah's tavern, it's Aunt Elizabeth's father's," Dorothy said crossly. Priscilla knew very well that the tavern belonged to Colonel James Stoodley, just as she knew that Dorothy's parents were dead and that her father's brother, Elijah Hall, who had married Colonel Stoodley's daughter Elizabeth, had taken her to live with them. But Dorothy always felt obliged to set things straight on the subject, perhaps, Priscilla thought, because Dorothy felt her hold on life precarious, orphaned as she was, and living on the bounty of relatives.

Priscilla understood about the precariousness of Dorothy's position. She herself had felt the ground fall away beneath her feet when her father had died so unexpectedly the year before, at the age of forty-two, leaving her mother with seven children to bring up. Gregory Purcell had been a sea captain and a merchant, with a shop on Long Wharf and a history of successful voyages. Before he married Sarah Wentworth he had built the fine house in which they all lived today. All of Portsmouth joined with Gregory himself in the expectation that he would go far, and that his energy and diligence would be crowned with financial success.

At the time of his death, his widow had been shocked to discover that she had been left in straitened circumstances.

"But how, Mother?" Betsy, then sixteen, wailed. "Father had been doing so well. He was forever telling us of it. Promising us a carriage soon almost as great as Mr. Atkinson's, and pretty clothes for all of us. Why was he prospering one day, and the next worth nothing but what was on the shelves of the shop, and much of that not yet paid for either?"

Sarah Purcell, her eyes red with weeping, had made a show of her Wentworth blood.

"Your father did not plan to die, Elizabeth. Nor did he mean that he would buy you today or tomorrow or the next day whatever he promised. In time he meant, if all should go well with him, to give us all those things. But this war, as you well know, has made a difference in our lives. Many things are hard to come by, and very dear if procurable at all. The war he had not counted on any more than he had planned on dying, I suppose."

"But what about the money Mr. Sherburne left to Father?"

"Oh, Elizabeth," Mrs. Purcell said helplessly. "It was not money at all, it was land only, and not even here but way over in Nottingham. Your father disposed of it almost at once, when you were six or seven. He needed money for a cargo and allowed he would not have use for acres of land twenty miles or more away since he had no intention of building a summer home nor a country estate as did Governor John. Make up your mind to it, miss, we are not in a very comfortable position. Well, we shall do the best we can."

The best they could do proved to be the opening, by Sarah Purcell, of a boardinghouse. Though a little frightened at what she was tackling, she proudly declined offers of help from her Wentworth relatives.

"Thank you, Cousin Joshua, I have made up my mind to manage, but I do thank you kindly." "No, Uncle Mark, we will not divide up our family, not just now, if you please. If we all work together, I think we shall succeed." "It is very generous of you, Mr. Atkinson, to offer to assist us in the name of dear Aunt Hannah, whom we still mourn. But, for now at least, we will try it my way. Perhaps we must accept help one day, but at first we will see what can be accomplished."

Not even her own parents were allowed to shelter some or all of the family in their house near the Puddle Dock, nor to help in any way, except for Sarah's "borrowing" of Caddie, her mother's old cook.

"With just your father and me at home, Caddie is bored with her duties," Grandmother Wentworth said to her daughter. "Or perhaps the lack of them. You know how she likes things lively. Her daughter Mussy has learned from her mother and will do well enough for us. You take Caddie. You will do her a favor, and us too, if the truth be known. But Caddie should still live with us, you know. You will not need her of the morning. She can go to you before midday, to prepare the dinner, and then to make supper for your boarders. Except for storms, she can sleep in her old room at home. It will work out very well for us all."

Grandmother Wentworth, Priscilla thought, had perhaps been more upset than anyone at the idea of having her daughter open a boardinghouse, but she had successfully hidden her feelings. Betsy, who was so thick with Sarah Wendell, had reported that Grandmother Wentworth had, in Sarah's hearing, said, "Genteel boardinghouse or no, it is not proper for a cousin of Governor John Wentworth to do such a thing."

But Sarah Purcell had had her way, and with Caddie to cook and two girls from the country to clean and serve, Mrs. Purcell very soon came to be known as an excellent boardinghouse keeper. When the Captain, who had arrived in July and settled in briefly at the Earl of Rockingham, had looked about for a permanent place to stay, he had fastened upon the Purcells'.

"I had not fancied to take roomers as well," Mrs. Purcell had remarked. "There being not more than enough room for myself and the seven girls, you might say, with space for the servants on the third floor. But he offered a handsome sum, and I own it is a comfort to have a man living in the house, so I told Captain Paul Jones he could come."

"Rubbish!" Betsy exclaimed gleefully, as soon as her mother was out of earshot. "Mother is under the man's spell, as is every other female in Portsmouth."

"Yourself excepted, of course," Priscilla had snapped at her sister. And that was true. Betsy had been, ever since Priscilla could remember, in love with Daniel Wendell, who, like Betsy herself, was now seventeen. Betsy Purcell would be as impervious as anyone could be to the charm of the Captain!

However, from the hour Captain John Paul Jones moved into the house, Priscilla felt her own life change. Almost every minute of the day there was the exciting possibility of seeing their important boarder. For one thing, he was a most interminable letter writer, and one never knew when he would hurry out of his room, having scratched away busily with his quill for hours at a time. In addition, he had innumerable things to do all day long. Mornings he frequently spent at Sheafe's Wharf, supervising the fitting out of the *Ranger,* the sloop he had come to Portsmouth to take under his command.

Priscilla's fast friendship with Dorothy Hall helped too, for between them they could keep careful watch on the Captain. When he wasn't dining or supping at Mrs. Purcell's excellent table, he could often be found in a corner in Stoodley's Tavern, where Dorothy could keep a round blue eye on him and report later to Priscilla.

"What we need," Priscilla murmured now to herself, unaware that she was speaking aloud, "is some new information. What little we know we have gone over together so many times." Dorothy reported to her faithfully enough, but she seldom, as she helped her aunt serve the food of an evening, picked up anything worth passing on. "Perhaps," Priscilla went on, talking softly into the gathering dusk, "I could approach him and say—"

"Miss Priscilla! With whom are you conversing? You are far from elderly enough to have developed the old ladies' habit of talking to yourself, I am sure."

Priscilla looked up into the glowing dark eyes and felt her heart jump up into her throat, where it began to pound mightily.

"Oh, I—"

The Captain laughed. He gently pulled her hand through the crook of his arm and said, "May we walk the rest of the way together, Miss Priscilla? And perhaps you will talk to me, instead of wasting your golden words on the evening breeze."

Priscilla blushed. How mortifying to be caught by the Captain—of all people!—talking to oneself. I can't wait to tell Dorothy about *this!*

"You are blushing, my young friend. It is very becoming and puts stars into those soft gray eyes. Never lose the ability to blush, Mistress Priscilla Purcell. It is a charming habit in a woman, and can soften a man's heart as can few other manifestations of emotion. Tears will do it sometimes, and yet often tears annoy a man, or even make him feel guilty. But a blush . . . When I am an old man, retired from the navy and through with the sea, I will write poems to blushes, I think. I will send you one. Would you like that?"

He's teasing me, Priscilla thought, feeling the soft wool of his dark-blue sleeve under her left palm. And she knew too that the Captain was treating her as a young lady and not as a child. Walking slowly through the gathering shadows they could have been any man and woman. This, in a sense, was her first truly grown-up moment.

I'll always be grateful to him for that, she surprised herself by thinking. Then she gave over to the pure joy of walking along Broad Street with Captain John Paul Jones, for all of Portsmouth to see.

Chapter 2

HE SAILS NEXT MONTH

S HE WAS late getting home after all, but when she entered the house with the Captain courteously holding open the door, her mother bit back the reprimand she obviously had waiting on her tongue, saying merely, "Hurry, dear, Caddie is in a state and you are needed."

Priscilla, her cheeks flaming and her eyes bright, fled to the kitchen. At the moment she wanted more than anything in the world to be allowed to climb up the long stairway straight from the kitchen to the third floor. She and Betsy had their room there now, as did the servants, ever since the Captain had taken up the big corner chamber, with the small dressing room behind it, on the second floor. Betsy complained bitterly about living with the servants, but Priscilla, remembering the reason for it, didn't mind. Now the small room with its dormer window seemed highly inviting. If only she could throw herself on the bed and relive every minute of that walk, remember the feel of the wool sleeve under her fingers, savor every single word! But Caddie was indeed, she saw at a glance, in one of her rare dark moods, and Mussy, Caddie's daughter, was in tears. Mussy, a pretty mulatto, had lately been keeping

company with Peter Gilman, and Caddie had let everyone
know that she did not approve of Peter, at least not for
Mussy.

"Mussy, are you not wanted at my mother's?" asked Mrs.
Purcell sharply, sweeping into the kitchen. "Priscilla, Jerusha has one of her headaches, and I sent Molly over to
the Whipples' to help tonight. They are having a party,
and are shorthanded. I thought we would be quiet here
and Molly not needed. The Captain is having a guest," she
went on, stealing a sidewise look at Caddie. Caddie, Priscilla knew, was charmed by the Captain, who often poked
his head into the kitchen to praise her.

"I have not had a dish like that since I was last in the
West Indies," he told her. Or, "I thought no one could
have such a touch with biscuit as my brother's cook in Virginia. If my Virginia plantation were not lying in ruins, I
would spirit you away to wait for me there. I dream I will
someday rebuild the place, and you are the first treasure I
will add to it," he told her gravely.

Caddie's dark face relaxed a trifle, Priscilla saw and
caught a quick smile from her mother. "Mr. Tilton and Mr.
Farnham are supping at the William Pitt tonight, and Mr.
Evans will be in Newcastle for another day or two, so there
will be only four—five," Mrs. Purcell went on. "Will you set
the table, Priscilla, please. Hannah and Mary are putting
the children to bed, and that may take some time. Meggie
is having one of her wailing fits. I am always so afraid the
baby will learn from her!"

Priscilla shook her head. "Susan is much too good-
natured," she said. "And sensible."

"Sensible—at one year!" exclaimed Mrs. Purcell. "Still, I
catch your meaning, Priscilla. She is a self-reliant sort of
baby, isn't she? Perhaps that is what comes of being born

after your father has died." She sighed, and Caddie, turning from the fireplace where she had just slung one of the
copper kettles on its crane, said brusquely, "Your children
is all good children, Mis' Purcell." Priscilla and her mother
saw with relief that the storm was, temporarily at least,
over.

"I suppose Her Majesty is over at Wendells'," Priscilla
said with a shrug. Even though Betsy was only a year
older, it did seem as though she had more privileges. Still,
there wasn't much use in complaining about having to
help around the house all the time, not now. After all, it
was where the Captain was.

She hurried into the dining room and began to set the
table for supper. Her favorite room in the house, in some
ways, the dining room had paneling of creamy white and
pale-blue wall paper with small white flowers. The tiles
around the fireplace were blue delft, brought from Holland
by one of Captain Purcell's ships long before, and represented scenes from the Bible. Above the mantel hung a
mirror, the mat around it embroidered by Frances, wife of
Governor John and now with him in England. When Mrs.
Purcell had come to the house as a bride, she brought the
blue-and-white chinaware that fitted into this dining room
so perfectly. It was a beautiful room, Priscilla thought,
carefully setting the table with the polished silver, the fig-
ured china, and the imported glass. Soon it would be echo-
ing to masculine voices and laughter as the Captain, his
guest, and the other boarders sat about the round table
and ate and talked and enjoyed themselves.

Priscilla's mother usually presided over the table at dinner, but supper was an informal meal and she knew her
male "guests" liked to be alone. Usually Molly or Jerusha
served, but occasionally Betsy and Priscilla were pressed

into service to deliver a steaming tureen or a second pudding to the table. Betsy quite frankly hated to do this, but Priscilla, although she felt self-conscious and all thumbs, welcomed the opportunity to see the Captain one more time, to hear his voice, to catch snatches of his stories that had their origins in so many far countries.

The table set, Priscilla gave it one last look and went to find her mother, who insisted on a final inspection.

"If we are to be known as having the finest boardinghouse in the town, and that is my intention," she had said, "we must be sure that everything is always just right."

Priscilla sniffed appreciatively as she walked into the kitchen. "Mm, chowder," she murmured. "The Captain's favorite. Smells wonderful, Caddie. Where's Mother?"

Caddie grinned happily and jerked her head toward the counting room across the hall. This was where Captain Purcell had kept his books, and it was used today by his widow for the business connected with the running of her boardinghouse. Priscilla found her mother poring over an account book. It was chilly in the little room. The sun seldom reached the windows of this northwest corner, which was shielded by a tall oak tree. The fire had not been lighted in the fireplace designed by Benjamin Franklin, the very same Benjamin Franklin who was today in France trying to enlist the help of the French in the miserable war. Dr. Franklin was a most remarkable man, it was said, concerning himself with the invention of odd contrivances. He had even, fifteen years ago, supervised personally the putting of a sort of stick on top of Captain MacPhaedris' imposing brick house, a stick that was supposed to prevent the lightning from striking the house and setting it on fire. People had laughed about that.

"Aren't you cold?" Priscilla asked, shivering at the

change from the warm kitchen. "I can light the fire."

"I'll be here only a minute or two," Mrs. Purcell said briskly. "No need to have a fire in this room, not until wintertime. I can always carry my ledgers into the parlor, if I need to. There, that's done." She opened one of the closets next to the fireplace and put the heavy ledger on a shelf. "Thank goodness your father had these closets built in every room," she said with a rueful smile. "He must have known he would have twelve children"—her voice faltered, but then went on "—or at least seven girls who would collect things like little squirrels. See down here?"

Priscilla looked at the lowest shelf and laughed. She recognized Mary's treasured wooden tea set, given to her by her grandfather on her tenth birthday just a few weeks before. Next to the tea set was a small battered tin chest from which spilled the clothes that belonged to eight-year-old Sarah's doll.

"How did they get here?" she asked. The children were not supposed to play in the counting room, which was kept clear for the calls of tradesmen. "Oh, I remember. There was a great fuss yesterday because Sarah purposely knocked Mary's teapot off the table. Mary said she would put it where Sarah could never find it. But how did Sarah's things come to be here? Or did Mary hide them too?"

"More likely Sarah, searching for the tea set, found it, thought it a fine hiding place, and moved in," Mrs. Purcell said. "Would you take the things back to the children's room, Priscilla?"

Priscilla gathered them up. "I finished the table," she said. "It's ready for inspection."

"I think we can dispense with the inspection," Mrs. Purcell told her with a warm smile. "You no longer forget the salt or the napkins or fail to count noses properly."

Priscilla seized the tin trunk and the tea set on its round wooden tray and ran up the wide staircase. Her heart was singing. This was the second time today she had felt grown up, and she found it exciting.

The rays of the sinking sun gilded the tops of the trees behind the house, and Priscilla paused on the landing, looking out of the small panes of the curved window. It was so peaceful outside, so calm and quiet. How could it be that the talk everywhere was of the stupid war? Such dreadful things going on, and yet on this golden afternoon the breeze was blowing across the Piscataqua River and Islington Creek, pushing away the threat of fog and clearing the skies to an enchanting blue.

She sighed, clutched the toys more tightly, and ran up the rest of the stairs to the room where Hannah and Mary had at last succeeded in quelling Meggie. Susan was already asleep, and Sarah was lying in her trundle bed humming one of her endless little tunes to herself. Priscilla put the toys where they belonged, smiled at Mary, who was playing cat's cradle with Meggie, looked at Hannah's impassive face, and left the room.

Hannah was a mystery to Priscilla. She never seemed to mind being with the younger children.

"Our Hannah is a born mother, I think," Sarah Purcell had said more than once, watching Hannah patiently caring for one small sister after another. "I hope one day she has a husband and a large family of her own to give all that love to."

Funny how different we all are, Priscilla thought, hurrying up the stairs to her attic room to make herself presentable. They all had smoke-gray eyes like their father's, and thick brown hair like their mother's, although Sarah's and Meggie's eyes were bluer than the rest, and Betsy and Sarah had hair that was lighter and more like Captain Gregory's sun-bleached blond hair. Priscilla remembered her brother Gregory well—he had lived long enough to become a person to her—and he had been a replica of the father for whom he was named. Martha she remembered slightly as having had her mother's blue eyes and fair hair. Abigail, Dorothy, and Mark she remembered not at all, and she sometimes wondered if her mother did. If so, was she glad that there were not more mouths to feed than the seven she was now accountable for? It was one of those things, Priscilla supposed, that you would never know.

In her room, Priscilla took a minute or two, after washing her face and hands and combing her hair carefully, to remember the thrill of walking along Broad Street with her hand tucked under the Captain's arm, of looking up into those dark smiling eyes. Priscilla herself was fairly tall, but she had the very strong impression of looking upward, even though their eyes could have been almost on the same level. He did that, creating the appearance of commanding height. It was a trick, she supposed, that came from the angle of his head and the way he looked at you.

There would be time later to think about the walk, and of course she would relive it again and again when she told Dorothy all about it, but now she was wanted downstairs. She ran down to the kitchen on the wooden staircase that was like a steep tunnel and found her mother and Caddie bustling about. The sounds coming from the door that led to the dining room told her the men had assembled and were waiting for their supper. Mrs. Purcell, looking pretty and poised in her familiar gray dress, had just come from greeting the guests, a courtesy she insisted on at all times, just as though she was the hostess and the men around her table invited guests, rather than paying ones.

"Priscilla," she said quickly, "can you manage this tureen by yourself? It is very heavy. Are you sure?"

Priscilla lifted the heavy tureen and started for the dining room. It took every effort to walk in and place it on the table without letting all those eyes know it was almost more than she could manage.

"Ah, one of Caddie's chowders!" exclaimed the Captain. "You must tell her for me, Miss Priscilla, how pleased I am. John, if you haven't tasted this delectable mess, you have a real treat in store for you." Priscilla turned uncertainly toward the kitchen. Her mother, just walking through the door, gave Priscilla a basket of hot biscuits to pass, while she herself seized the heavy porcelain ladle and began to serve the chowder into deep wide soup plates.

Priscilla stole a look at the Captain, but after a quick and courteous nod at her mother, he returned to his conversation.

"Although I have not been told much more than that, I can only conclude, as I'm sure you all do—I know at least that John agrees with me—that a certain victory is in the wind. I have hoped to be appointed the courier that will carry the news to Mr. Franklin and Mr. Adams in Paris. The *Ranger* is ready to go, or will be in a few days. And the *Ranger* will speed the news to the place where it will do the most good, to our ambassadors who are trying to arrange the French alliance."

"When should you set sail, Captain Paul Jones?" asked little Mr. Mason. He was a small, soft-spoken man who always sounded as though he was whispering.

"I hope by the fifteenth of the month, sir," Captain Jones said. He shot a look at John Langdon. "Perhaps sooner. Perhaps sooner."

By the look of him, it couldn't be too soon, Priscilla

thought resentfully. He might be a horse just out of the stable, ready to run as far and as fast as he could. Then she realized what he had just said, and what it meant. The Captain was leaving. Leaving Portsmouth, leaving her house, sailing away to France on the *Ranger*. She had always known it was coming, because that was what he was here for, but—next month!

She let go of the basket she was holding, and it fell to the floor, bouncing gently. The white cloth slipped sideways, and the two remaining biscuits rolled on the carpet, still steaming.

"There are plenty more in the kitchen," Mrs. Purcell said calmly. "Fetch them, please, Priscilla." She finished ladling the chowder, and Priscilla made a hasty exit. She wasn't sure, but she thought she had seen an understanding twinkle in her mother's eyes.

Next month, she mourned to herself as she flung the dropped biscuits into the fire petulantly. Next month. What will I do? What will we all do—without him?

Chapter 3

THE TINGLING AIR

THE WORD was quickly all over town. "Uncle Elijah says that the sailing itself is common knowledge," Dorothy reported. "After all, the Captain has been promising the men action. But the reason for the delay—that, my uncle thinks, is supposed to be kept quiet. He is very much disturbed, my uncle. One might as well put a piece in the *Gazette,* he says, as tell that mealymouthed little Joseph Mason anything."

"Mr. Mason has just come to town—the Captain wouldn't know that," Priscilla said, defending the Captain stoutly.

"I know, and you know. Well, the damage is done. The exciting part of it, Uncle says, is that the news will be good, or so they hope. That is what they are waiting for, you know."

"I don't see how they can know," Priscilla grumbled. But she had great respect for Dorothy's uncle. He had been working on the *Ranger* when the Captain had come to Portsmouth to take her over, and Captain Jones had only praise for Elijah Hall. It came as a surprise to them all, even Dorothy, when her uncle announced that he would sail with Captain Paul Jones on the *Ranger.*

"My Aunt Elizabeth is beside herself," Dorothy announced dramatically. "She tries to tell him that Colonel James is unable to run the tavern without help. But Uncle Elijah merely laughs at her and says she is of more assistance to her father than he will ever be. Besides, he's been at the shipyard on Langdon's Island all this time, working with Mr. Hackett on the *Ranger* and the others, and she didn't carry on so about *that!* She just likes to grumble, I suppose. *I* think it's thrilling."

"So do I," Priscilla agreed. "He will write home to your aunt, will he not? So we will have constant news of—of the *Ranger*."

"Of the Captain, you mean," Dorothy commented with a wink. "But I agree, Pris. Now we will know what is going on. *If* they ever go," she finished with a scowl.

"Go!" wailed Priscilla. "But we don't want him to go!"

For nearly three months her life had been centered on that one figure. And now the figure was to remove itself from the picture. She couldn't understand Dorothy's attitude. Dorothy, she guessed, was more interested in worshiping at the feet of a hero than in having the man around. But then, Dorothy saw him only at the tavern, sitting at table with other Portsmouth notables. She had never paced along the street with him, her hand tucked into the bend of his arm.

Priscilla was meditating on this as she walked home. She had left Dorothy's reluctantly. Tonight there was to be a ball at the tavern in the arched hall on the third floor. As usual, Dorothy would be standing, half hidden, outside one of the doors, watching the fun. There would be dancing and light chatter, and Cuffee, General Whipple's slave, would be fiddling away for dear life. Later in the evening Cuffee might be joined by Colonel Michael Wentworth, who could, if he felt like it, play his violin until dawn. How often Priscilla had begged her mother to be allowed to stay overnight at Dorothy's, to peek in on the belles dressed in their finest and the men elegantly clad, all whirling about at the public dance, but the answer was always the same. Her eyes looked ahead to the darkening street, but her mind was behind her on the upper floors of Stoodley's Tavern.

"Is there a ghost pursuing you?" Priscilla jumped nervously and turned. The voice was familiar and not familiar, just one of the voices she had heard in her life that made little impression on her. "Or do you prefer to run? A fellow is hard put to follow you. Or maybe you wish to discourage company?"

"Oh, Mark." She recognized him at last. Mark Jaffrey had been around ever since she could remember, on the outer circle of her life. He had lived in Newcastle until a few years before when his father had died. His mother had at once remarried and moved away, Priscilla had heard, to Salem. Mark had gone too, at first, but one day he had turned up at the Whipples' next door to the Purcells'. There he seemed to work for his keep, doing odd jobs and studying, when there was time, under Colonel Whipple himself, who liked to encourage education in the young. The house was not so close as to enable the two households to see much of each other. Furthermore, Sarah Purcell had always been much more friendly with Molly Shortridge, who lived two houses away. Whenever Sarah Purcell wanted to borrow something, or wished to seek advice, or had a desire to chat, even, it was to Molly that she turned.

Priscilla had been aware of Mark living next door at the Whipples', but that was all. He had been a tall thin lad with sharp features and soft brown eyes. "Cow eyes," Dorothy had called them once, giggling, as the two girls compared notes on boys and girls they remembered from the days before they were so well acquainted. But now, as Priscilla looked at him in the half-light, she saw that the eyes had a certain pull to them, and that the sharp features were no longer protruding from a bone-thin face, but had become, almost, handsome.

"I—I didn't—how are you, Mark?" she said at last stiffly, knowing something was expected of her.

"I am very well, Miss Priscilla Purcell, I thank you," he said gravely, and she saw a twinkle in the dark eyes. "Now that we have dispensed with the formalities, will you tell me if you are running from a ghost, or simply filled with an urge to run, or if you saw me behind you and wished to elude me?"

"I didn't see you, and I don't know any ghosts, nor do I—Perhaps," she finished at last, "I was just in a hurry to get home."

"It is growing dark," he agreed gravely. "Well, Priscilla, I will protect you, if you'll let me."

He bent his arm, crooking it toward her, and she automatically slipped her hand through the bend, thinking with a pang that the only other time this had happened it had been—him.

"Thank you, Mark," she said solemnly. Then some of her mother's instructions came faintly to mind. "Tell me about yourself," she said courteously. "Are you still living at the Whipples', and—"

"Oh, Priscilla Purcell, you cut me to the quick!" he said, laughing. "I have not been living at the Whipple house for near a year now. And you haven't even noticed my absence!"

"I'm sorry, Mark. We have—we have been busy," she said.

"I know. And I haven't seen you to tell you, Priscilla, but I was sorry about your father. A fine man, and a great loss. Especially to you and your mother, of course, but so well thought of in town."

"Thank you, Mark," she said quietly. "But—well, where do you live now? I mean—"

"I live at the Livermores'. You remember the tale of John Sullivan, who did the chores about the place, reading law in his spare time? Then he defended someone who had been in a fight, and was so good at it as to set his client free? Well, Mr. Livermore was so pleased on that occasion that he told John Sullivan to stop carrying wood for the kitchen and grooming the Livermore horses and all that, and to give the law studies his undivided attention. Mr. Sullivan did well, as everyone in Portsmouth now knows. So Mr. Livermore then decided to encourage more young men to become students, and I am his latest," he finished proudly.

"But, Mark, that's wonderful," she said sincerely. "You will be a judge then?"

"With any luck at all, a lawyer at least," he said modestly. "When I get back, we will see."

"Get back? You are going away? To college, perhaps?"

"No, Priscilla. No one has seen fit to give me the money to attend a college, I'm afraid. But I thought you might have guessed. I'm to sail with the *Ranger,* when she leaves Portsmouth."

"The *Ranger?* You'll go with the Captain?" Priscilla gasped. "Oh, Mark."

"I can think of no one better to sail under," he said sharply. "I'm sure he will be an inspiration to us all."

"Oh, yes, of course, Mark. He—he is—well, everyone knows he is a fine officer. It's just that—well, I didn't know—"

"I have only just signed," he said quickly. "Perhaps the very last to do so. It was not an easy decision to make, although I have less to lose than most. And it is, I suppose, one way to see the world."

"Yes." Priscilla looked searchingly into his face, seeing there for just a moment the thin-featured boy he had been, with a lost look to him that she had forgotten all about. "You must tell me everything you see, when you come back, Mark."

"Could I—would you let me write to you, once or twice perhaps?" he asked. "I have no family, you know. My mother has married a new husband and is starting a second brood. She has forgotten me, I think."

"Of course she hasn't! But please do write to me. I'll look forward to your letters."

They had reached the gate to Priscilla's house, and she walked across the dusky square of garden to the door feeling a kind of throb in her throat. Why couldn't I have said something—really nice, really warm, she thought. But he surprised me so—

Priscilla was wrapped in her thoughts as she went into the house. Without looking about her, she walked slowly toward the staircase, and for probably the first time since July, she started to climb the stairs without so much as glancing toward the door of the Captain's room. A sound finally cut through her consciousness, a sound of weeping. Almost in a dream, Priscilla turned toward her mother's room and the hiccuping sobs that came from behind the white door. She rapped timidly with her knuckles. It was not her mother who was weeping. Who, then?

Mrs. Purcell glanced up quickly as Priscilla walked in, then made a brief warning gesture. Priscilla looked at the figure on the bed, and saw in amazement that it was Betsy, flung on the quilt like a rag doll, weeping uncontrollably. Betsy, who never cried, who never seemed to have any emotions at all, for that matter, except where Daniel Wendell was concerned . . .

"Daniel?" Priscilla mouthed at her mother, and Mrs. Purcell, with a slight shrug, nodded. Then she said calmly, and loudly enough so that Betsy could hear the words between sobs, "Daniel, along with so many of our patriotic young men, has signed on the *Ranger*. It is exciting, don't you agree, Priscilla? Elizabeth will think so too, when she has stopped remembering only herself."

Betsy turned her tear-soaked face toward her mother. "Of course I'm thinking about myself," she cried, sniffing and mopping at her cheeks with a damp handkerchief. "Why shouldn't I? Daniel is my whole life, and you know it, and yet I'm not supposed to care that he is going away? Maybe forever?" The sobbing commenced, and Priscilla stared at her sister in distaste.

"Of course you're supposed to care. We all care," she said sharply, aware that she had never spoken to Betsy this way before. "Daniel is one of many, after all. Everywhere you go, you hear of someone who is leaving too, but I don't believe all of the women are making such—such spectacles of themselves. I hope not anyway."

"They probably don't feel as I do," Betsy said. "I have thought of nothing but Daniel ever since I can remember."

"Ever since any of us can remember," Mrs. Purcell said, with a grim smile. "I can see that this disgraceful conduct may be my fault. I should never have allowed you to spend so much time at the Wendells'. You have lost your sense of values as well as your dignity, and I'm ashamed of you, Elizabeth Purcell. I am indeed. What would your father say?"

"Perhaps she'll stay home and do some work around the place now," Priscilla suggested and immediately regretted her sharpness. There was no doubt at all that Betsy's misery was genuine. "Oh, do cheer up, Betsy. Daniel will love every minute of it. He will see the world, and he will have a chance to serve under the Captain—"

"You and your precious Captain!" wailed Betsy. "It's all his fault. Sarah told me that her father had persuaded Daniel not to think of going, but Captain Jones strolled over to talk to him and within five minutes Mr. Wendell had agreed to Daniel's leaving. He's even written a letter about Daniel that Captain Jones is supposed to deliver to Dr. Franklin when he gets to—to Paris." The thought of distant Paris reduced Betsy to sobs once more.

"But why Daniel?" Priscilla asked her mother. "I mean, he is a nice enough person, but why should Dr. Franklin concern himself with Daniel Wendell?"

She had thought Betsy too thoroughly engaged in her grieving to hear, but Betsy's ears had ever been sharp where Daniel was concerned, and she lashed out, "Why not Daniel? After all, he is cousin to John Hancock and John Adams, and to the Colonel Quincy in Braintree the Captain spoke so highly of the other day. He has unusual connections besides being a Wendell and a Wentworth, and he is—he is—Daniel!" she finished in another wail.

Mrs. Purcell smiled at Priscilla. "John Wendell is, perhaps, Captain Paul Jones's best friend here in Portsmouth. It's only natural, I think, that a proud father should use his influence to further his son's career."

"Career!" Betsy sat up on her mother's bed, pushing her

hair back from her forehead and staring wildly. "Career? But Daniel isn't going to be a—a common sailor. He's— well, he's going to settle down right here in Portsmouth, and—and—well, be a merchant or something."

"Did he tell you so?" Mrs. Purcell asked gently. "Or is that just your picture of him, Elizabeth?"

From the stricken expression on her sister's face, Priscilla guessed that her mother had hit uncomfortably close to the truth, and she was shrewd enough to realize that here, right in front of her now, might be the reason for Betsy's hysterical reception of the news of Daniel's departure. If they were promised, as Priscilla had secretly thought them to be, Betsy would be sad, of course, but a little proud. Wouldn't she? But now she saw Daniel slipping from her grasp forever.

Mrs. Purcell suddenly stood up. "Elizabeth, wash your face. And, Priscilla, your hair wants smoothing. Then I need you both in the kitchen. Mussy is warring with her mother over that worthless beau of hers again, and I told Caddie she could take the evening for herself, to see if she could straighten matters out. Mothers," she added with a smile, "have their troubles."

"Come on, Betsy. Supposing Daniel should walk into the house and see you looking like this!" The words had an immediate effect. Betsy's hands went swiftly to her hair and twitched at her wrinkled skirt. "I'm truly sorry," Priscilla added to her sister, as they started up the stairs to their room. "But—well, if you stop to think about it, half the men in town are either away somewhere right this minute or they are going away. You heard the Captain the other night. He said there were more than three thousand men from the Province of New Hampshire engaged in privateering alone, and of course this is the only harbor, so naturally a big number of them is from here. And—well, there are the regiments that went out from here after the fighting in Massachusetts two years ago. Many of those men are still fighting somewhere, even if they don't get much food or have decent clothes to wear. At least Daniel will be on a fine new ship, under the greatest commander in the country, so everyone says. That is something, isn't it?"

Betsy, who had been splashing her face vigorously with cold water, nodded slowly. Her nose, Priscilla noticed, went up proudly as it always did when she spoke of Daniel.

"I suppose so," she said in a natural voice. "Yes, I should have expected it. Daniel will be a midshipman, you know. Sarah told me about the letter her father wrote. I think he hopes for an early promotion for Daniel, to lieutenant perhaps. I suppose Captain Jones, because of his friendship with Mr. Wendell, will see fit to promote Daniel at once. Sarah says that a kinsman of theirs, named Simpson, will look after Daniel if Captain Jones should quit the *Ranger.*"

"Quit the *Ranger!* Why ever should he? It's his ship!"

"Oh, he has other fish to fry, Sarah says."

"Sarah says. What does she know?" Priscilla asked haughtily.

She wasn't very fond of Sarah Wendell, partly, she supposed, because Betsy set such store by her, but mostly because Daniel's older sister seemed to be forever looking down her nose at one.

"If anyone knows what is on Captain Jones's mind, Sarah does," Betsy proclaimed, brushing her hair with long, sweeping strokes. "He may be the most run-after man in the Province, but everyone knows where his heart is engaged. You should see him look at Sarah."

Priscilla's heart sank. "Pooh, he looks at everyone that

way," she said curtly. "Besides, her father is his best friend. You said so yourself. Or Mother did."

"You wouldn't be jealous of Sarah, would you?" Betsy, her good nature completely restored, grinned impishly and ran down the stairway to the kitchen. Priscilla turned to the washbowl, noticing glumly that either Molly hadn't filled the pitcher to the brim, or Betsy had used more than her share of the water. Probably both. She did the best she could with the small amount remaining in the heavy, pink-sprigged pitcher, and as she washed, she thought of Betsy and Daniel.

What would it be like to have someone sail away on the *Ranger*? She could imagine the white sails filling as the ship turned slowly and headed for the Atlantic Ocean, leaving the Piscataqua River and the fine harbor it afforded Portsmouth. She could picture the crowds waving, a few women crying quietly, men climbing up among the spars of other ships in the harbor to wave good-by and call to the friends who were sailing. Betsy would be there, waving to Daniel.

And I? I'll be there too, waving for all I'm worth at the Captain. I—and a hundred other women, no doubt. A thousand, more likely! She smiled wryly. Then she remembered Mark Jaffrey, who had slipped entirely out of her mind from the moment she had entered her mother's bedroom.

I will be there waving to Mark! she thought. He wants me to be there. He came here to tell me so.

Then it was her turn to run down the stairway to the kitchen. Her feet, she was sure, were like her heart, suddenly lighter because someone had sought her out. Even if it was only Mark Jaffrey, a lad who meant nothing to her, it was pleasant to know she was in his mind at such a moment.

Chapter 4

A GIFT FOR THE CAPTAIN

MARK JAFFREY may not have been the last to sign on with Captain Paul Jones, but he was one of the last, because the news was suddenly all over town that the complement of the *Ranger* had been filled. It was also known that the *Ranger* was ready to sail, but that, for one reason or another, orders had not been given.

Although the Captain had stated at dinner and had repeated elsewhere that he was waiting for news of some kind, rumors flew about the town.

"He is going to take an ambassador to France," they said. "Dr. Franklin and Mr. Adams are to be replaced. After all, they have been there for near a year, and nothing has been accomplished. They want replacing."

"These things take time," others objected. "They are good men, perhaps the best this country has to offer. And Silas Deane too. The *Ranger,* more like, is to carry men to help them, or plans from the Congress in Pennsylvania. Or money."

"Not money. We have sent the men to Europe to *borrow* money because we have none. No, there must be another reason for the delay."

Priscilla remembered vaguely that the Captain had spoken of "a victory in the wind," but it meant little to her. Whatever the reason she hoped it would remain an obstacle to the sailing, although even she found herself enjoying the excitement in the air these days.

The Captain might be depressed and moody, but the rest of the town seemed aroused to a fever pitch. The young men who would go with the *Ranger* were stopped on the street, given messages to carry to relatives and friends on other ships in other ports, invited to supper, forced to accept small gifts of caps and stockings. Even though young men had been leaving town steadily for a year or two, there was something particular about this group, and Priscilla knew with pride that it was because of the Captain. Everything the Captain was concerned with immediately developed an air of its own.

The excitement at first blew around in a great gusty storm, unsettling them all, but after a week or so it began to break down, in a way, into smaller separate eddies. A group of women her mother's age began a frantic campaign to find cloth to make warm coats for the men who would be crossing the Atlantic in the brisk November and December breezes. The women at church were concerning themselves with finding boots for them, since all available leather had been used long ago to put boots on the feet of those who were marching in the wilderness. Hides were found and men to tan them and finally men to cut and stitch the boots as quickly as possible.

The Captain was gravely grateful for these attentions.

"The navy," he said, "has become forgotten in the scheme of things. No wonder, with two thousand privateers on the seas, and only something like twenty naval ships either afloat or, most of them, still in the yards, without stores or arms. So it is most kind of you, *mesdames,* to think of my men, and I thank you heartily on their behalf, as well as for myself."

Mrs. Cutt, who had presented to the Captain the clothing she and the others had assembled, blushed crimson.

"We have all," she said quickly, "done as much for the men in the army, as you may know. Our regiments, however, were not badly off when they left here."

"I know," the Captain said gravely, but there was a twinkle in his black eyes. "Your regiments were the pride and joy of the late Royal Governor, and they were well trained and well equipped, thanks to his interest and his efforts. After the battles at Lexington and Concord they marched away in his fine uniforms, carrying muskets bought with his money, to fight against his cause. But by now they will have need of your help, and I hope, *madame,* they are as grateful as I am for your generosity."

This little scene had taken place in the Purcell parlor, where the ladies were shown when they came to call upon the Captain and to bestow their gifts. Priscilla, with Dorothy, hovered in the doorway and listened unashamedly, smiling as the Captain's graceful acceptance washed smoothly over the heads of the delighted ladies.

The parlor, with six women and the Captain in it, seemed to have shrunk. The Indian shutters, put there once for protection from the Indians when that sort of protection was needed, had been closed against the gathering dusk. The "courting lamps" on the mantelpiece, whose short wick burned down quickly, reminding a courting visitor to go home, had not been lighted. But there were candles on the spinet, and a fire burned low in the big fireplace. Normally, Priscilla knew, her mother would have seated herself behind the polished mahogany table to give her guests tea poured from her shining silver pot, but there was no tea to spare and no one expected it now.

It was like a painting, almost, the firelight flickering on the glowing faces and dull wool garments of the ladies, the Captain's dark head and black eyes gleaming in the fitful light. Then the women stirred, with a little sigh, and one by one inclining her head to the Captain, stealing one more look into his attentive eyes, they left. Priscilla closed the front door behind them and watched the Captain slowly mount the stairs to his room. The charm and fixed attention she had noticed in the parlor had dropped away. He seemed a man who was weary, weary of waiting, perhaps, because he did little enough these days.

Dorothy was standing in front of the fireplace, holding her hands out to the blaze.

"Your mother said to tell you she wouldn't need you for a while," she said. "He seems tired, Pris. Doesn't he?"

Priscilla nodded slowly and began to put the chairs back into their usual positions.

"I think he has what my Grandmother Wentworth calls 'tiredness of the spirit,'" she said. "When we were little and dawdled when she thought we should be hurrying to get outside, she would say, 'Is it fatigue of the body, children, or tiredness of the spirit that I see?'"

"Yes, I see what you mean. It is hard for such a man to be kept dangling, I suppose. Even Uncle Elijah is fair crazy with the delay, and yet my Aunt Elizabeth keeps him so busy it's a wonder to me he can remember, even, that he is supposed to be leaving soon."

Dorothy sat down on a chair near the fire, and Priscilla dropped onto the old chest.

"I wish we could give him something," she said. "Don't you? Some little thing, I suppose, because what could you and I do for him? I guess it's silly, but—"

Dorothy gave Priscilla a level stare.

"Why, no, I don't think it's silly. As a matter of fact, and I'd forgotten it until this very minute, I was going to ask you to come to my place tomorrow afternoon. Helen will be there, and Caroline Chandler, and I suppose Anna will tag along . . ."

Dorothy made a face and Priscilla laughed. Helen Seavey had been a close friend of Dorothy's until a few months before. She had lived in a little house down Daniel Street, not far from Colonel Stoodley's tavern, and Helen and Dorothy had been friends for reason of geography more than anything else. Helen, two years older than Dorothy, had been married in May to a young officer in the New Hampshire line who had left for the front almost immediately. Helen Seavey had come back to live with her mother, but because Dorothy and Priscilla were now always so busy together, the two girls had not picked up their friendship. Helen had, Dorothy reported, become friendly with Anna Hilton, a plain girl who was also a neighbor and whom Dorothy detested because she was always so unhappy and complaining.

"But what has that to do with a gift for the Captain? Or with me?" Priscilla asked idly. "How does Caroline Chandler fit into that group? Or do I, for that matter?"

Dorothy shrugged. "Helen has something on her mind and it concerns the *Ranger,* that's all I know. I suppose, if you'd just been married and then your husband had marched away with the army you'd be looking for things to do to keep busy. Her mother's house is tiny, you know, it is nothing much to keep it clean. As for Caroline, she and Helen used to be friends, and I suppose they are again. Anyway, Helen called on us this morning and told me she had an idea about the *Ranger* and would like to have me, and you and Betsy, and—"

"Did she mention me? By name, I mean?" Priscilla had thought Helen Seavey didn't know Priscilla Purcell was alive, and she was pleased.

"W-well no," Dorothy said reluctantly. "Not by name, Pris. But she said, 'Your new friend and her older sister.' She meant you, there's no doubt of that."

"But what does she want of us?"

"She wouldn't tell me. But she sounded very important and a little mysterious too. I'm dying to find out what it is. There may be others, perhaps Mary Langdon, she said, and—oh, I don't know. Anyway, she said she had some sassafras and we could make sassafras tea, since no one has any real tea, of course. Aunt Elizabeth said she would manage something for us to eat, since Helen was doing that much. At three o'clock, she said, and that is a good time for you as well as for me. Will you tell Betsy, Pris? And now I must go."

"Betsy won't come," Priscilla said. "She doesn't go anywhere but to the Wendells'. Especially now."

"Perhaps she will. Helen and Caroline are more her age than ours, and Helen's husband is in the army, while Caroline's intended is at Mr. Langdon's shipyard but will be in the army soon. Betsy will like being one of these widow-like creatures, who rock and sigh and read bits of their lovers' letters out loud."

Priscilla giggled. "I think you know my sister better than I do," she admitted. "How are you so wise?"

Dorothy shrugged. "Ask her, anyway. You know, Pris, I really feel sorry for Betsy. I know I've teased her, and sometimes I've thought her a silly girl to run after Daniel Wendell so that the whole town knows about it. But it's real to her, isn't it? I mean, she suffers just as much as Helen or Caroline or any of them. Maybe more. How do we know? Uncle Elijah says some people can stand pain better than other people, if they burn their finger or get shot, he means. Perhaps it's the same way with having a pain in your heart. Well, I must go, or Aunt Elizabeth will have much to say. She is cross these days anyway, because of Uncle Elijah leaving so soon."

Priscilla was in her room mending a torn hem before her mother should spy it, when Betsy walked in slowly. She had that look of despair so common with her lately. Priscilla, who had already made up her mind to be kind and gentle with Betsy, after Dorothy's unexpected little speech, felt her heart harden.

"Oh, don't look so—so deprived!" she blurted out. And before Betsy could do more than throw her an astonished look she added, more softly, "I have an invitation for you," and went on quickly, relaying Dorothy's invitation.

Betsy heard her out with a stony face. "I don't want—"

"Helen's husband is an officer in the army, as you know. And Caroline Chandler is engaged to that Vaughan fellow —you know who I mean. He was hurt at the rope walk a while back. When his leg is right, he will enlist too. You should really, Betsy, make some friends to share your grief with, you know."

Betsy favored her sister with another outraged stare, and then unexpectedly she giggled.

"Perhaps you're right," she said. "I know I have had about enough of Miss Sarah Wendell. She is beginning to treat me like a servant. And besides—"

Besides, Daniel won't be at the house much longer, so what's the point of going there? Priscilla added silently, but aloud she said, "Three o'clock tomorrow. Don't forget."

Even Betsy seemed a little excited, Priscilla thought, as they set out the next day. Priscilla's own heart was pounding, although she couldn't imagine why. She was only going to Dorothy's, after all, a thing she had done two or three times a week ever since July or early August. But today was different. They were walking, she suspected, into one of those little eddies of excitement she had noticed around town, little whirlpools of people gathered together for one reason or another but all related, in some way, to the departure of the *Ranger*.

Betsy was looking around her as though she had never been in this part of town before.

"You told me about Caroline and Helen," she said. "Of course I know your little friend. But who else will be there?"

"Anna Hilton will be coming."

"I don't know her."

"I don't either. Dorothy does, although not very well. I know who she is to look at, but I've never said two words to her. She is very plain and very poor and always sorry for herself, Dorothy says. Dorothy can't abide her."

"She sounds charming. Who else?"

"Maybe Augusta Peirce, I think, but I'm not sure. Oh, and I think Dorothy said something about Mary Langdon."

"Mary?" Betsy's face brightened. Mary Langdon was one of the prettiest girls in Portsmouth, and these days surely one of the wealthiest. Priscilla found that she too hoped Mary Langdon would be there. She had long wished to know her better.

The sisters quickened their steps as they crossed The Parade, but as they reached the walk in front of the tavern they unconsciously slowed down. Betsy, to Priscilla's surprise, hung back, letting her younger sister take the lead. It was a new experience, and Priscilla wasn't sure she liked it. Somehow she had expected to hide behind her older sister's skirts, instead of boldly leading the way into the tavern.

Dorothy was waiting for them. She had on her next-to-best dress, Priscilla noticed, wishing she had dressed up a little herself. It was then, even for Dorothy, an occasion.

"You're the last," Dorothy said, giving Betsy a warm welcoming smile. "We have this little room here."

She led them into a dark, low-ceilinged room. There were pewter plates and mugs spaced on a cup rail, and a small fire burned in the deep fireplace, its faint light complemented by candles burning in wall sconces. Priscilla glanced around quickly. Her eyes first lighted on Helen Seavey, a tall, rather heavy brunette, who was standing with her arm resting lightly on the mantelpiece. She wore a dark-red dress that glowed in the golden light. Her dark hair, piled on her head, made her look even taller than she was, and her brown eyes were warm and friendly. She inclined her head toward the Purcell sisters gravely and then looked back at a piece of paper she held in her hand, studying it closely.

"You know Caroline Chandler," Dorothy said. Dorothy, Priscilla thought, was doing very well. Only Priscilla would guess that she was at all nervous and flustered by the duties of hostess. She gave Dorothy an encouraging nod and looked at Caroline Chandler, a willowy blonde with a very white skin and curiously light eyes. Caroline nodded and smiled and said nothing. "And Augusta Peirce?" Augusta was a plain girl with heavy features and thick, rough hair. When she smiled, as she did now, her face seemed to change entirely, and she was no longer plain, but animated and almost pretty.

Priscilla blinked at the transformation, and her eyes moved on to Anna Hilton. The sharp little sallow face, the close-together dark eyes, the tightly drawn back hair, were just as she remembered, and in this case there was no smile to turn a plain face into a pretty one. Priscilla ducked her head in acknowledgment and turned to the last figure in the room.

Mary Langdon was sitting, as though it was her due, in the only comfortable chair in the room, half reclining with her white arms lying gracefully along its arms. Her golden head was back against the cushion, the firelight picking out glints in it here and there. Her large blue eyes looked lazily into Priscilla's, and the red lips curved into a smile. Priscilla felt herself catching her breath. How beautiful she is! She realized that for the first time in her life she was seeing someone to whom that word applied.

"Are we all here now?" The deep, musical voice was Helen Seavey's. She looked around the group and then turned to face them more squarely. "I suppose, since I called this meeting, so to speak, I had better explain why we're here." Priscilla slid down onto a wooden settle beside Dorothy, watching Betty slip into a straight chair in the corner. "I think you all know, really, what this is all about. So many people have been doing things for the *Ranger* and for Captain Paul Jones and the men he is taking with him. And just by chance I have heard what the Captain really wants. As far as I know no one has thought of it—at least we hope no one else has the same idea. Because we want to give it to him ourselves."

"Give what?" Betsy asked, and then shrunk back into the shadows as she realized it was she who had asked the question.

"Wait a minute. Let me read you something." Helen

picked up the piece of paper she had been studying, turned it over, frowned, turned it end to end and said, "Mr. Fowle let me copy this from the *Gazette*. It is quoted from the *Journals of Congress* of June 14, 1777, and it reads: 'Resolved, That the Flag of the thirteen United States be thirteen stripes, alternately red and white, that the union be thirteen stars, white in a blue field, representing a new constellation.'"

She looked around the upturned faces.

"On the very same day, and also in the *Journals of Congress*, there appears the appointment of Captain John Paul Jones to command the *Ranger*, with a description of the *Ranger*, number of guns, and all. I have been told that the Captain himself marked the coincidence of the two things appearing in the Records on the same day, and he said, 'We are twins, the flag and I.' So, there is just one thing for us to do."

She made another of her dramatic pauses, her dark eyes sweeping the circle slowly.

"But don't you see?" she exclaimed impatiently. "The Captain wants a flag for the *Ranger*. We will make him one. It's as easy as that."

There was an excited murmur as the girls thought it over and began eagerly to speak. Priscilla sat motionless, aware that Dorothy was chattering away, but not listening to her. It had all been said too quickly. The idea was new, and she had absolutely no inkling of what the flag would look like, because she hadn't listened. All she knew at the moment was that the Captain was to sail away in the *Ranger* with, flying from the mast, a flag which she herself had helped to make.

It was too wonderful to be true.

Chapter 5

THE QUILTING PARTY

B UT WHAT WILL it look like? How will we know how
to make a flag?" Dorothy asked at last. Priscilla was relieved, and she thought the others were too. Probably no
one wanted to ask the question, but Dorothy had always
been outspoken. Perhaps having the others in her own
home gave her a feeling of confidence.

"This is what it will look like," Helen said briskly. She
turned over the sheet of paper in her hand. "Mr. Fowle
and I drew it from the description I just read you. These
shaded stripes will be red, of course, and this square is
blue. The other stripes and the stars are white."

"But how do you know the stripes go that way?" Caroline Chandler objected. "Perhaps they're supposed to go
up and down, Helen."

"Mr. Fowle tried that, and we agreed it didn't look
right," Helen said definitely. Everything Helen Seavey said
was uttered with authority. How could she know so much,
or be so sure?

"We should have another flag to copy," Augusta Peirce
suggested. "You can't be sure, Helen. Not even Daniel
Fowle knows everything."

"There is no flag to copy," Helen retorted impatiently. "There is no such flag in existence, don't you see? That's why it's so important. We will make the flag, the very first flag of our colonies ever!"

There was a silence, an uneasy silence filled with doubts and misgivings and, at the same time, excitement. At the end of it, five or six voices broke the bubble of quiet all at once.

"How do we know the size?" "Who knows how to make a flag?" "Is it silk, do you think, or cotton?" "Or wool?" "The Captain could tell us, let us ask him—"

For a moment Helen Seavey watched them with a patient, almost maternal air. At last she made a little signal for silence.

"It is to be made of silk, because that is durable as well as light," she said firmly. "I have already talked to Mr. Sheafe and a couple of others who know about such things. I think one of you just now suggested speaking to Captain Paul Jones about it. No indeed, this is to be a surprise for him. He has been given much in the last weeks, I know, but this gift is bound to charm him the most. I'm sure of it."

Mary Langdon stirred and looked around. Her blue eyes were shining and her face was even more beautiful when it was animated and sparkling.

"We must run right out and buy the silk then!" she cried. "If we can but just figure out the quantities we will need. Oh, Helen, what a splendid idea!"

Helen shook her head. "You know we can't run right out and buy silk," she said shortly. "Although we do have the measurements. I have taken care of that myself."

Mary tossed back the blonde curl that fell on one shoulder, and her lips pursed into a pout. Mary was not used to being crossed. At that moment Dorothy put her mouth close to Priscilla's ear and muttered, "Helen always did want to be the general of the army. I had almost forgotten," and Priscilla repressed a giggle.

"Then how can we make a flag?" Anna asked in an unpleasant tone. "If it must be of silk, and we have no silk? Really, Helen!"

"We will make it of what we do have," Helen told her calmly. "Of our petticoats and dresses, whatever we can find. Isn't it worth a small sacrifice, girls?"

Everyone began to talk at once. After casting an anguished glance at Betsy and muttering, "There aren't many spare petticoats hanging in Purcell cupboards," Priscilla was silent. She looked around at the circle of protesting faces again. Except for Mary Langdon, who never seemed to lack for pretty clothes, she doubted if any girl in the room had, lying about, odd lengths of silk, still on a bolt or made up into unwanted dresses or petticoats. Certainly not Anna Hilton. Nor Augusta Peirce, to look at her. And if Caroline was getting married, she would be treasuring every scrap of material for her trousseau.

"I, for example," Helen went on, drawing herself up as tall as she could and looking at them all with a challenging gleam in her dark eyes, "can provide much of the white silk for the stripes. Perhaps all of it. I plan to use my wedding dress."

"Your wedding dress!" They gasped the words in unison. Sacrificing an everyday dress, or even a Sunday-best would be difficult. But a wedding dress! They looked in awe at the only married member of the group. How could she so much as think of such a thing? "Oh, Helen, not your wedding dress!"

"Why not? I know it is the custom to keep it, to have

one's daughters marry in it, and their daughters after them. But—well, this is war. I may not have daughters at all, and if I do, I'm sure they would rather find their own wedding dresses, knowing that their mother's had gone into the very first flag this country ever saw!"

The girls nodded gravely. For the first time they were aware of the importance of the moment. Until now it had been a lark, merely tea-party chatter, but Helen, with the sacrifice of her wedding gown, had made the creation of the flag into a matter of great importance.

"Caroline, that blue-silk cloak of yours—I know, it will be impossible to replace it now, because of the war and the empty shelves in the shops—but, well—you can manage, can't you? It would be perfect for the blue field, behind the stars."

Helen spoke gently, but Priscilla sensed, behind the calm words, the implication of an order. Caroline Chandler made a face. Her white skin turned pink and her light-blue eyes narrowed.

"If someone will explain to William," she said with a shrug, "why the future Mrs. Vaughan will come to him without a cloak to her back, I think I can manage. I have my old gray, which Will says is the color of the mud on Christian Shore and which is fit only for stormy days. Perhaps we can arrange for bad weather from now until the end of the war."

They laughed, a sympathetic ripple of laughter that tried to tell Caroline how much they appreciated her sacrifice.

"Mary, you showed me the red ball gown in which you made such a dazzling impression on Boston last month. It would be exactly right for the stripes, of course."

Mary sat up stiffly and stared into Helen's dark eyes angrily.

"My beautiful red dress! But I've only worn it that once, Helen Seavey!" she cried. "It must last me for—for years, you know that, unless the war is over and the ships start bringing in goods again."

"You have many dresses, Mary Langdon," Helen said shortly. "And all pretty, I imagine. Oh, I know John Hancock himself said you were, outside of his wife, the most beautiful woman in the colonies, and I know your red dress contributed to the picture that you made, but—we need red silk, Mary Langdon. And you know it."

Mary pouted again, but her blue eyes sparkled as she remembered. Priscilla had a momentary vision of Mary, her golden hair piled high on her head, her rustling, shimmering red gown billowing around her feet, the brilliant hue setting off the whiteness of arms and neck. She imagined Mary dancing with the elegant Mr. Hancock and listening to his praises. It would be hard, she thought, to give up such a dress. But if Helen could part with her wedding gown—

"I have—I have some red silk!"

They turned and stared at Anna Hilton, who was sitting on the edge of her chair and looking eagerly at Helen. The sallow cheeks were crimson with embarrassment, and the deep-set, dark eyes looked as though tears were about to well up into them.

"It—it was brought to me by my uncle, on his last voyage," Anna said, the words spilling out as though she couldn't prevent their being said although she would like to. "The last one before he was lost. He bought it for me because—because when I was little I used to say I wanted red shoes and a red dress, and he thought—he said—" The stream of words ceased suddenly, terminating in a little sob. "It is a very pretty red," she added quietly. "Bright. It is very fine Chinese silk. I am sure there would be enough,

Helen, because it has not been cut, you see, but is still rolled up, waiting for—for me to have it made up into—"

There was a deep silence in the room, broken only by the snapping of the wood in the fire. Priscilla cast around desperately for something to say, to break the silence. It was almost more than she could bear hearing Anna—who had so little, who had nothing, really—offer her single treasure.

Helen found her voice at last.

"Anna, my dear, that is very generous of you. And I—"

"Oh, Anna, I was a beast!" Mary Langdon stood up and leaned against the mantelpiece beside Helen's tall figure. She looked up into Helen's eyes and shook her head, then she leaned down and touched Anna's cheek lightly with her forefinger. "I have been spoiled and selfish all my life," she said. "I have been ashamed of myself before, but never so much as now. Of course we will use my red dress, girls. I have worn it once and had an evening in it such as I may never enjoy again, who knows? It is so much better to keep the memory and lose the dress, than to take away from someone else the fun of—of knowing such an evening is ahead. Keep your silk, Anna, and someday you will wear your pretty dress and remember how close you came to never having it."

Priscilla had been swept along by the rush of words. She wasn't quite sure what Mary had said, but she did know that the girl whose blue eyes glittered with excitement and, possibly, tears had been enormously tactful.

"Whew!" breathed Dorothy in Priscilla's ear, and Betsy threw an understanding smile in their direction.

"That's settled then," Helen said briskly, and Priscilla was glad that the moment was over. She could tell from the expressions of relief in the ring of faces that the others were glad too. "And Anna, we all thank you. But Mary is right, her dress has had its day." She looked around, from face to face, ending at last with Mary Langdon's, so close to her own. "Would tomorrow suit you, girls? Only earlier—much earlier—at one, say? Dorothy, may we meet here again, do you think? I'm sure none of us have rooms that are large enough, or unused, or suitable for our purpose. We will need a table, a large one, for cutting on, and Dorothy, does your Aunt Elizabeth have some sharp shears we can use, and Mary, would you—"

My goodness, she does like to be the general, Priscilla thought. But I suppose someone has to give the orders, and since she has appointed herself anyway, it will be Helen Seavey. She half heard additional instructions—"Please bring any scraps of white silk you may have. I am sure my dress will supply the stripes, although some of them may have to be pieced. We can get a few stars from the sleeves and perhaps from the bodice here or there, but I'm sure we will need more. Any white silk will do. And thread, please everyone bring thread and your own needle. And some white cotton."

"Cotton?" Dorothy asked. "Why do we want cotton, for heaven's sake?"

"The stars must be quilted," Helen replied firmly. "We will need bits of cotton for that."

Priscilla and Dorothy exchanged amused glances. Both Priscilla's mother and Dorothy's aunt had been threatening to force the girls to learn how to quilt, and they had so far successfully resisted the efforts. Now it would appear that they were going to learn in spite of themselves.

"Oh, well, it's in a good cause," Dorothy muttered with a chuckle. "I believe I even look forward to it, this way!" As Priscilla nodded, Dorothy stood up. "Come help me,

Pris," she said in a low voice, and added in a louder tone, "I think we should have our tea now. Helen brought it with her, you know, although it's only sassafras."

"We have a little. Real tea!" exclaimed Augusta eagerly. "I will bring it tomorrow. That is, if anyone wishes me to."

"Real tea? Augusta, really? That would be heaven," Mary Langdon cried. "And I will provide some little cakes our cook makes out of practically nothing."

Priscilla looked back at them from the doorway as she followed Dorothy to the kitchen. In the flickering light of the fire, she thought even Anna looked almost pretty, engaged in eager conversation with Mary Langdon.

"Somehow," she murmured to Dorothy as they put cups and saucers on a big tray to carry back to the others, "I feel that more has been accomplished today than a plan to make a flag. Do you too?"

Dorothy nodded solemnly. "I guess," she said philosophically, "that's what happens when people get together. It's the war that does it. At least Uncle Elijah says that, terrible as it is, the war has made a difference in all our lives. The Captain being here in Portsmouth, for example. Anna for once doing something besides complain. Mary Langdon admitting that she's spoiled and selfish. It's the war, and growing up, and—and just living, I suppose. Here, I'll carry this if you'll hold the doors for me on the way. Ready?"

Priscilla had enjoyed the hours spent that afternoon at Colonel Stoodley's so much that she looked forward to many more. Even Betsy said she hadn't had as much pleasure in a long time, and she had no complaints at all now about having been included in the group. So it came as a disappointment for the sisters to discover that the flag was to be finished much sooner than they had expected. Except for a few stitches here and there, it was actually to be completed the next day.

For one thing, with her usual efficiency, Helen had given Mary Langdon careful measurements, so that Mary arrived at the tavern the next day with her stripes carefully cut and ready to sew. Helen had cut her wedding dress into the needed white stripes. Had it been difficult for her in the end, Priscilla wondered, looking searchingly at that strong, calm face? She had not only made a pattern for the stars, but had succeeded in cutting three from what was left of her own white silk. Priscilla, Dorothy, and Betsy were able to fashion the remaining ten from the white-silk petticoat Augusta had brought with her. Caroline, with Helen's help and with one last melodramatic sigh and feigned sob, slashed into her blue cloak and achieved a fine square of blue. Next she joined Anna in cutting from the bits of silk contributed by Anna and the Purcell sisters a second set of stars for the reverse side of the field. Dorothy and Priscilla found themselves taking lessons in quilting before they knew it, and Priscilla stitched away happily, glad that it had fallen to her lot to work on a star instead of the more tedious stripes.

"Does she have to keep at us so?" Betsy, also sewing a star, muttered under her breath, and Dorothy, working between the Purcell sisters, answered reasonably, "You know perfectly well, Betsy Purcell, we'd have these stars floating all over the sky if she didn't show us exactly where each one is to be placed."

When Priscilla finished her first star, she looked at it critically. "It's not very smooth," she said worriedly, examining the stitches taken by Dorothy and Betsy. "But yours aren't perfect either."

"No one is going to be looking at our flag to see how well it is made." Helen, who seemed to be everywhere at once and at the same time always sewing, reassured her. "And I know you'll find the next one will go along more smoothly, Priscilla. But in the meantime, why don't you sit next to Augusta and work on a stripe?"

Priscilla blushed and threaded her needle once more before she took her place next to Augusta. The flag had been taking shape rapidly as they worked. Stripes were sewn together, seams felled, then pairs of stripes were neatly joined. As soon as one girl had finished a long seam on red and white, she was moved to work on a star, then called back to help out with another stretch of felling. The constant moving about kept them from becoming bored as well as easing cramped muscles and relieving tired eyes.

All the time she was sewing as rapidly as she could on the joining together of two pieces that consisted of four stripes each, Priscilla found she was longing to get back to her second star. It would be, she promised herself, so much better than the first. When at last she surrendered her large red-and-white rectangle to Helen, she sat down eagerly between Mary and Caroline at the blue square. "Is that the top, Mary?" she asked and let her eyes move carefully along the circle. This, she counted to herself, is number seven. How wonderful—my lucky number! Someday the Captain will say to me, "Every time I looked at my new flag I watched the seventh star. Did you make that one, Miss Priscilla?" And I will tell him yes. The seventh star. Perfect!

Her second attempt at quilting did, as Helen had prophesied, go much better. By the time she had finished the seventh star, Priscilla had managed to forget that she had sewn the first one, which still looked wrinkled and clumsy

to her, although no worse, she thought, than the first attempts of the others. This one, she was determined, would
be perfect. Even if one were to spread the flag out on a table, looking for flaws in it, she was determined that he
would find no mistake in the seventh star. She stitched and
dreamed and didn't listen to the chatter around her. It was
almost as though she was sewing into the white five-
pointed bits of silk a special message. Or perhaps, she
thought wistfully, a little good luck. If only she could tuck
a lucky piece of some kind inside and stitch it down securely. Or a prayer, perhaps, a prayer for victory and a
safe return . . .

The October afternoon had nearly come to an end when
Mrs. Hall bustled into the room exclaiming, "Girls, girls,
you will have no eyes left. See how dark it is outside.
Threatening to storm, I'm sure, and you sewing away here
with a dying fire and but two candles. I'm ashamed of you
all. What your mothers will say of the hospitality at Stoodley's Tavern I can't imagine. My husband was just now
bringing a lamp, but I think I saw Captain Jones on the
street, on his way here, and no doubt the lamp will be forgotten. I will go fetch it myself or make him come here at
once." She hurried toward the door, but Helen Seavey,
moving quickly for a person so large and placid in appearance, caught her arm.

"Please, Mrs. Hall, please do wait a minute. You haven't
told her?" she demanded of Dorothy.

"You asked me not to."

"I know. But perhaps she should know. It was kind of
you, Mrs. Hall, to allow us to use this room a second time,
especially since you did not know what we are up to."

"Why—why, sewing, I see. Something for the soldiers, no
doubt, your husband's regiment, Helen?"

"No. See here." Helen, with one of the dramatic gestures that seemed to come to her so naturally, picked up the blue square with its circle of stars now almost quilted into place, and put it down in its rightful position next to the brilliant red and white stripes. "It is a flag, Mrs. Hall," she said proudly. "A flag for the *Ranger*. Please do not tell your husband, it is to be a surprise for the Captain. For all of them."

Dorothy's Aunt Elizabeth was a short, plump woman with dark hair and darting birdlike eyes that were now fastened inquisitively on Helen's face. At the mention of the *Ranger*, Priscilla saw a scowl gather on the low forehead and watched the small mouth pinch itself into a straight line. But when the bright little eyes looked down to where Helen's hands held the silken material together, a transformation took place on the round face.

"A flag," Mrs. Hall breathed. "A flag for the *Ranger*. Why, girls, the Captain will be that pleased. And my husband too." She stared at the flag thoughtfully for a moment. "And my husband too," she repeated slowly. "I won't tell. You shall have your surprise." She walked out of the room.

"I think somehow she has decided to forgive Uncle Elijah," Dorothy whispered to Priscilla. "I think she's forgotten about that lamp too. But no matter, I'll get one. Shall we have tea first, Helen, and finish afterward?"

"Let's work half an hour more," Helen said swiftly. "Do you all agree? Then I can finish anything that needs to be done at home. Dorothy, why don't you and Augusta make the tea, since it's your house and her tea, and the rest of us will stitch away as fast as we can. Perhaps it will all come out even."

"Yes, General," Dorothy muttered and Priscilla, who a

moment before had been conscious only of the fact that the Captain might be within a few yards of her, bent to her stitches with a smothered giggle. Dorothy left with Augusta, and Priscilla, squinting to see better in the dim light, took the final stitches in her star.

"I'm done," she breathed, and almost at the same time she heard Betsy cry with a sigh of relief, "That's finished!"

"Mine too. What else can we do?" asked Mary Langdon.

"That's all, then." Helen pushed back her dark hair with a tired smile. For the first time Priscilla was conscious of the work Helen had done the evening before to be ready for this afternoon. She looked around. Mary, in spite of Helen's words, had joined Caroline to help her finish hemming the blue field. Caroline, with her tongue between her teeth, had continued to stitch on the ruin of her blue cloak. Anna held the work very close to her eyes, but sewed doggedly on the last gay stripe. Betsy was scowling at the star she had just finished. Last of all, Priscilla turned her gaze to Helen, who looked exhausted to the point of dropping. The generalship had done it, Priscilla reflected. Helen had kept at them unceasingly, moving them from task to task to prevent boredom, organizing the work so that eight girls could, with a minimum of fuss and with little interference, work together in a small space and even stitch simultaneously on the same pieces of material.

"It's done, girls, except for the hems along the sides and whipping the corners so that they will be firm. The ship's sailmaker will finish this end, he has a device for making and binding the holes, Mr. Fowle told me. It's been a good day's work, I think. I hope you feel so too. We must make plans for presenting it to the Captain. Perhaps Dorothy, when she returns, can help us by finding out from her uncle what is scheduled, if he knows and if he'll tell. I'll—I'll let you know. Because we must all give the flag to the Captain, all of us. It should be a sort of—ceremony."

Priscilla, who always found herself ready to criticize Helen whenever she became domineering, lapsed into quiet appreciation. A ceremony. The occasion wanted just that, a ceremony. They must come to our house, Priscilla thought, since the Captain lives there, and make him a present of this flag. In our parlor. It will be like the ladies giving the Captain the clothing the other day. Only this time it will be us, our little group, and he will be thanking us.

"On board the *Ranger*, of course," Helen went on. "I believe Dorothy's uncle must be let in on the secret after all, because he can arrange it for us. We must go aboard the *Ranger* and present the Captain—and it—with our flag."

Chapter 6

THE EVE OF SAILING

I T IS USELESS," Betsy remarked, slapping the sheets on the bed with unnecessary violence, "to tell that Helen Seavey anything. She will do it her way, and there is no other. Dorothy Hall seems like a nice sensible girl. I don't know how she could be such friends with her for so long."

"Dorothy said Helen always did like to play general," Priscilla admitted, "but then, as Grandmother Wentworth always tells us, no one is perfect, not even oneself!"

The sisters finished their mother's room and moved on to the adjacent room with its row of small beds. Daily tasks were strictly regimented in the Purcell house. Betsy and Priscilla felt that, as the eldest, they were given more than their share of work, but neither of them ever dared rebel or skimp on her duties. Priscilla often wished that, since once-a-week airing and changing of beds fell to Betsy and herself, the Captain's room had been included. She wanted to roam about in the spacious bedroom and smaller dressing room, to see and touch his belongings. But Mrs. Purcell had been firm about having Molly and Jerusha take entire care of their roomer's quarters.

Usually she and Betsy carried on their chores in silence.

It now struck Priscilla as odd that they were having, for once, a perfectly normal and sisterlike conversation. All because, she supposed, of the two afternoons spent at Stoodley's, and because for the first time in years she and Betsy had gone somewhere together. That and Daniel's immediate departure from Portsmouth, for all at once Betsy had ceased her constant attendance at the Wendell house and was actually speaking unkindly of Sarah Wendell.

So, Priscilla thought, smoothing the blankets on Meggie's trundle bed with a practiced hand, it all goes back to the *Ranger* and its sailing, which they say can happen at any time.

"I know I have lost my argument before I have so much as made it," Betsy said, pushing the trundle bed so violently that it rolled under Mary's cot and out the other side. She giggled and jerked it back into its rightful position. "Haste makes waste, I know. Please don't remind me again of what Grandmother Wentworth would say. Come to think about it, why am I hurrying? When we started, I had some idea of planning a party of sorts, asking Mother to get Caddie to make a molasses cake, if we have any molasses left, and inviting Captain Jones and—well, giving him the flag. The Captain lives in our house, why should Colonel Stoodley's be mentioned in the *Gazette* yet another time?"

Priscilla bent over the sheet she was folding to hide a smile. So that was it! She had wondered at Betsy's burning desire to hold the presentation ceremony in the Purcell parlor. Now she understood. Out of friendship for Helen, Daniel Fowle might see fit to print a little item about it in the paper, and of course Daniel Wendell would see it there. Perhaps he would even cut it out and carry it next his heart!

"Helen has already told us," Priscilla said, "that we should give the Captain his flag aboard the *Ranger*. And I think we should. Aren't you dying to see the ship anyway, Betsy?" She stole a sidewise glance at Betsy's stormy face. "After all, it's where Daniel will be living for weeks and weeks, you know. Maybe longer."

"Y-yes," Betsy agreed doubtfully. "But just the same, I don't see why Helen Seavey has the say about everything."

"The flag was her idea in the first place, so why not? There, that's the last. Mother will be surprised, we have done the rooms in record time." And the sisters went on to their next assignment.

The Captain was not present at the midday meal. Afterward Betsy and Priscilla were helping Jerusha and Molly clear up when Dorothy came running into the kitchen.

"It is all settled. Everything has come out even. Isn't that wonderful? Because we were so worried for fear there would be no time, or that for some reason he would say no, it was impossible, but he has agreed, and without asking a single question."

"Which is more," Betsy commented dryly, "than can be said of us. Of me, at any rate, because I intend to ask several questions. Just take a deep breath, Dorothy, before you turn black in the face what with running every step of the way here and talking all at once. Tell us slowly what it is you are trying to say."

Dorothy sank down on the settle, untied her bonnet strings, and unclasped the cloak fastened under her chin.

"I'm sorry," she said at last, "but all the way over I was wondering just where to begin. I guess I never did find the answer, so I began with everything, all at once."

"You did indeed," Betsy assured her. "Here is a bit of custard left over from dinner. Eat it, and then tell us."

Dorothy obediently spooned custard into her mouth, and after the first mouthful or two she began to eat more quickly.

"Don't gobble," Betsy reproved her. "We're in no hurry."

"Perhaps you are in no hurry, but I am. There, that's enough, Dorothy. You eat too many custards and puddings at home, you told me so yourself." Priscilla took the dish from her friend's hands and stood in front of her, arms akimbo. "Now, Mistress Hall, if you please."

Dorothy smiled at them both, her blue eyes twinkling.

"The custard calmed me down well, as you intended," she said demurely. "Now, here is my message. The Captain cannot sail tomorrow, as he planned, and—"

"Tomorrow!" The sisters gazed at each other, but Priscilla saw the Captain's dark face rather than Betsy's, and she knew that Betsy was, in her mind, looking at Daniel.

"No, because there is such an east wind, and that will not do, although the Captain is angry because tomorrow is the last day in October and he had promised himself and his men that they would sail 'this month.' Still, there is nothing for it but he must wait another day, when the wind will surely change, everyone is sure of it."

"Dorothy, you are rattling on again," Betsy complained. "Is she always like this, Pris?"

"What about the—the flag?" Priscilla prompted. "When do we give it to him?"

"Tomorrow. In the morning, at eleven o'clock the Captain has agreed to receive us aboard. Helen thinks he must know, or at least suspect, what it is we have to give him— he has so readily accepted the suggestion that we make the gift on the deck of the *Ranger*. I didn't dare say so to Helen, but I would not be surprised if perhaps Uncle Elijah said a word or two to the Captain. Helen would be furious."

"She need never know. If she did find out, she should be glad, not furious, because with all the fuss and bother of boarding the men and sailing so soon he might refuse to see us at all."

"Yes, that's true." Dorothy looked about her for the first time. "I do like this kitchen, ours is so big and so—so busy all the time."

"You have more mouths to feed. Oh, was the Captain at your tavern this noon? He wasn't here." Priscilla always liked to know exactly where the Captain was every minute, if she could manage it, although, she thought with a pang, in a day or two there would be no more keeping up with him.

"Yes, eating a broiled lobster as though he hadn't a care in the world! I saw him in conversation with Uncle Elijah in a corner, in that same room where we were sewing," Dorothy said. "I thought nothing of it at the time—they always have their heads together, to my Aunt Elizabeth's annoyance, of course. Then Helen came over and seized me by the hand as though I were a child, and dragged me to Captain Jones. Uncle Elijah politely disappeared, and Helen asked him. And he said Yes."

"Asked him what?"

"Why, she said she and I and a few other friends had a gift for him and she asked permission to give it to him aboard the *Ranger* at his convenience. She still had hold of my hand, and I could tell from the way she clutched my fingers that she fully expected him to refuse. Instead he smiled that beautiful smile, and he bent his head in that little nod, you know what I mean, Pris? He said, 'Young ladies, it will be my pleasure to receive you aboard my ship tomorrow morning. Would eleven o'clock suit you?' "

Betsy snorted gently. "You children and the Captain,"

she chided them. "Do the others know, Dorothy?"

"Helen has gone herself to tell Mary," Dorothy said.

"Mary, of course," Betsy murmured.

"—And she sent Augusta to tell Anna and Caroline. Oh, dear me, what shall I wear? I can't think. First I decided to wear my blue, but Aunt Elizabeth would never let me wear it of a weekday morning, no matter what the occasion. The green, which is still good, is rather light for the last day in October, but the brown is so—so dull."

Priscilla rapidly reviewed her own meager wardrobe, and she knew that Betsy's mind moved in the same way.

"Helen says she will wear that same dark red, that it is all she has now but her best dress, and that would not be right. Besides, she said she wore it to make the flag in, and that gives it sentimental value, but I call that silly of her."

"No," Betsy said slowly, wrinkling her brow. "I think I see what she means. If she tells the others the same thing, that will prevent Mary from wearing one of her dazzling new outfits, and it will make poor Anna feel better. The Purcell girls too! Let us wear our Quilting-Party costumes too, Pris, for sentimental reasons only!"

"Why did you say Helen thought the Captain knew about the flag? Did she say so?"

"Yes, as she left she said to me, 'Captain Paul Jones wasn't even curious about his gift, was he? Perhaps he is weary of receiving gifts and is too polite to say so. Or perhaps he somehow knows what it is.'"

"Did she seem upset?"

"Not a bit. She was glowing—you know how she is when she's pleased? She is so handsome then! She was delighted to have him agree to see us. But I must go back. Aunt Elizabeth is getting into a state of nerves again, now that it is so close to the time for Uncle Elijah to leave. I think perhaps I can help to calm her down. Maybe I should give her some custard!" Dorothy gave her high giggle, smiled at Pris and Betsy, and fastened her cloak quickly. "The flag meant something to her, did you notice that? I believe it—it sounds foolish, perhaps, but it made Uncle Elijah's leaving less of a whim on his part, more of a mission, a worthwhile mission perhaps."

After Dorothy had run out into the cold, gusty air, Betsy and Priscilla worked in silence, putting the blue-and-white china away neatly in the pantry, getting the kitchen ready for the preparation, a few hours hence, of the evening meal.

"The flag could mean that, to Dorothy's aunt," Betsy said slowly. "A flag is a symbol, is it not? It stands for something. And this one stands, I believe, not only for the *Ranger* and the Captain and Daniel and the other men on board, but for—for the cause, in a sense. For freedom, and independence, and for our victory. I never thought of it that way, when I was taking those tiny little stitches and hoping no one would see how uneven they were. I was thinking more of Mary's red gown, and Helen giving her wedding dress—I could never do that, never, never, never —and mostly of Daniel looking at it sometimes and remembering me."

"I know." Priscilla felt tempted to mention the seventh star, but she thought better of it. "Me too, Betsy. But I see what you mean about the—the meaning. Do you suppose Helen saw it like that all the time?"

"Perhaps she did," Betsy said solemnly. "She is older than we are. She is married. Perhaps her thoughts are deeper than ours. I'm sure of it, Pris."

At supper that evening the Captain was alternately pale and preoccupied, jovial and loquacious. Jerusha had one of her headaches, and Molly, whose current admirer was to sail on the *Ranger*, had, without asking permission, left the house to see him. Mrs. Purcell was occupied in the nursery with Margaret and Susan, who had colds and were fretful. So Betsy and Priscilla were pressed into service in the dining room, to Priscilla's delight and to Betsy's annoyance. For Betsy had determined to swallow her pride and go to call on Sarah Wendell, meaning Daniel, once more. Their mother, however, had been firm, and Betsy was reduced to sulking.

"No one in there pays any attention to what he eats," she muttered, cutting squares of hot johnnycake with quick jabs of her bread knife. "Least of all your precious Captain. He just sits there, either saying nothing or spouting away endlessly."

When Priscilla carried the platter of golden squares into the dining room, the Captain was holding forth in a long humorous monologue that had the other three men at the table apparently spellbound. A few minutes later, his tale over, the Captain once again lapsed into silence, his eyes brooding and withdrawn.

"He has been packing all day," Priscilla said in his defense, "and hurrying around town doing last-minute things. He must have much on his mind, with the final loading and all."

"Then why doesn't he go to his room or somewhere and do his worrying?" Betsy cried shortly. Priscilla looked thoughtfully at her sister. For some time Betsy had shown no signs of temper or despair. Now it was as though, with word that the *Ranger* would at last leave Portsmouth, all the thoughts she had put out of her head came crowding back to torment her.

And crowding back into my head too, Priscilla thought with a pang. Except for a few minutes in the morning she might never see the Captain again.

"Betsy, run over to Wendells'," she said gently. "I can manage the rest by myself. Truly I can. Mother need never know. If she does come down, I will tell her it was all my idea."

"Oh, Pris, I—" Priscilla saw tears welling up in her sister's gray eyes. "I really shouldn't, but I—"

"Run," Priscilla said firmly. "Besides, this way I can be near the Captain twice as much, don't you see?"

Betsy clutched gladly at the line Priscilla had thrown her and was gone in a moment. Caddie looked up from the sauce she was making for the Captain's favorite dessert and smiled at Priscilla.

"She is unhappy now, that one," she rumbled in her deep voice. "Wait for him to be gone, then she know what unhappy is."

Priscilla nodded, suddenly close to tears herself. She watched Caddie spoon the velvety sauce over the mounds of pudding and put the plates on a tray. So much emotion all at once. Yet ever since Sheriff Parker, dressed in his old-fashioned coat and cocked hat, had read the Declaration of Independence from the balcony of the Court House nearly two and a half years ago there had been emotion not only in Portsmouth but all over the young nation, she supposed. Before that, even.

Someone had been affected by the war one way or another ever since. Now it touched the Purcells. It was not, she thought, like the time her father had died. That had been the deepest sort of grief, but it had been private and personal. Now they were caught up in the same mesh that entangled so many families—and it was little comfort to know that others were sorrowing tonight too.

"But why am I so emotional about it?" Priscilla asked

herself crossly, preparing to lift the heavy tray. "The Captain is—the Captain. He is nothing, really, to me. Not a figure in my life, as Daniel is in Betsy's, or Jed in Molly's, or —or any of them."

The tray was too heavy for her. She brought it to an abrupt rest in the pantry and carried the plates two by two into the dining room. The Captain was talking again, and she listened as she walked around, eyes downcast, filling cups and making sure that each guest had the proper silver.

"I will spread this news in France in thirty days," he was saying in his most ringing voice. "I told that to the Governor and the others when they came to speak to me earlier today, and I say it again to you gentlemen now. The word of Burgoyne's surrender at Saratoga may well be the final push that is needed to talk the French into an alliance with us. Once we have ships and men and supplies, and above all money from the French, the British will be on the run. We have been waiting, as you know, for this victory. Some of our men have seen it coming, although I must admit to those of us languishing here miles from action it has at times appeared much too remote, and too long about getting here. But now we have it, the Congress has asked me to carry the news to France, and you have my word, the entire country has my word, that it will be cried aloud in Paris in thirty days. The east wind will not hold forever, and I have a fine fast ship, good men, and the strong breezes of victory to help me on my way."

So that was it. Priscilla withdrew to the pantry, but stood there out of sight, expressly against her mother's orders. Mrs. Purcell had forbidden eavesdropping on the guests ever. Priscilla wished, suddenly, for Betsy to talk to, or even for her mother. Wanting action at least, she de-

cided to send Caddie home, telling her she would finish up
for her in the kitchen. Instead, she stood there in the pantry, irresolute, uncertain, feeling life pulsing and fluttering
about her and wondering if she had a place in it, or if she
was forever destined to lurk behind a door, listening, not
taking part.

A slight noise hard by stirred her, and she turned
quickly to the big tin tray, pretending to be fully occupied
with putting it down on the shelf.

"Miss Priscilla," said the familiar voice. She turned,
wondering if it showed on her face or in her eyes, this de-
scent into the depths she had just taken. "Ah, you too are
sad. Do not be, do not be." The Captain looked at her and
as always she had the impression he was looking down
from a great height, and yet their eyes were almost level.
"The whole town, the Province, the world, is sad tonight.
Yet for the first time, the curtain has been lifted. No one
seems to understand that, and of course it is because for
so long things have been much too black. Now there is
light at last. Tomorrow or the next day you and all the
others will begin to see and understand."

Priscilla stared at him helplessly. Is he telling me this,
she wondered dully, or himself? Or is he rehearsing a
speech to give to some desolate mother, perhaps, or to—
well, to Sarah Wendell, or one of his other admirers?

"I believe," the Captain went on in a gentler tone, and
this time she knew his dark eyes saw her, not some page
of history, "that you are one of those who will grace the
deck of my ship tomorrow, Priscilla? That is so? Good. I
had hoped to invite you aboard in any case, you and Miss
Betsy, and of course *madame* your mother, if she could
come. I am glad you will be there. You will, perhaps, bring
luck to my ship. I think it is more than possible."

Priscilla thought of her star, and the lucky piece she had wished to sew securely inside, along with the fluff of cotton.

She smiled and said sedately, "I hope so, sir. I wish you luck. We all do."

"And my men? No doubt there is one among them who means something a little more to you than the others?"

"Oh, n-no," Priscilla stammered, thinking: If he only knew!

"Ah, I see that pretty blush again, that so-becoming blush! But I have discussed that with you. Then there is one lad on my ship who will be in your thoughts, as we sail? That is good, I would not have it any other way, Miss Priscilla. I suppose you won't tell me his name? No? Then I must ferret out your secret for myself. I will, you know. Now I must see Caddie, and thank her for her many fine dishes, and assure her I will be back one day for more. And you, my child, I will see tomorrow, on my *Ranger*."

Priscilla stood motionless as he went into the kitchen, then she hurried into the dining room, seized a handful of plates, which she dumped unceremoniously on the tray and carried out to the kitchen.

Tears were rolling down Caddie's fat black cheeks and in her hand she held what could only be, Priscilla thought shrewdly, coins. Yes, the Captain would thank Caddie in other ways, considering honeyed words not enough. She saw the slight figure make to Caddie as graceful a bow as he would bestow on Dorothy Quincy Hancock, whom he so greatly admired. He turned. At that moment there was a sharp knock, and almost at once the kitchen door flew open. Priscilla, turning quickly, saw a stranger standing there.

"Priscilla," said a voice. "Don't look frightened. It is only

I, Mark Jaffrey. I—Captain, sir, I did not see you!"

"I am just leaving," Captain Jones said easily. "Good evening, Jaffrey. I will leave you to your farewells. There is no one, I believe, in the parlor, Priscilla. My tablemates all left at once for the William Pitt, I heard them discuss a meeting there. I am going to my room for my last few minutes of preparations, for I will sleep aboard tomorrow. Miss Priscilla, I will see you in the morning at eleven. And you, Mark Jaffrey, I will see earlier. And later. And for many a day."

He bowed again, this time to Priscilla, and as he raised his head, the dark eyes flashed her a gleam of amusement. A gleam of knowledge too. So this is the one, they said. Now I know.

Priscilla stared after him. No, she wanted to cry, you are wrong. Mark is nothing, really. But she looked up at the tall young man beside her and thought, I couldn't say he is nothing. He is a person, very much a person, and he has come to tell me good-by.

"You run long, Miss Prissy," Caddie said, in her deep, rich voice. "I clean up here."

Only a few minutes ago, Priscilla had meant to come and say almost those very words to Caddie.

"Thank you, Caddie," she said with dignity. "Come with me, Mark, and please don't look around you. We are a little upset today. But of course, so is everyone else in town, isn't that true? Mark, I am so glad to see you!"

Chapter 7

A FLAG FOR THE *RANGER*

BUT THEY CAN'T all be here because of—of us!" gasped Augusta.

Priscilla turned to Augusta and smiled reassuringly. "I know how you feel," she said. "I wondered about it too. Then I realized that almost everyone in town has someone sailing on the *Ranger*. Or if not, has a relative or friend on one of the other ships in port. They have come down for one last inspection. Look!"

She gestured around the harbor. There were masts reaching toward the sky at every wharf and dock. Small figures were swarming on spars, scrubbing decks, dangling on ropes along dark hulls as they scraped and painted and washed. The Piscataqua was alive with ships and men. Along the shore, scattered in small clumps on every wharf, were men and women and children come down to welcome home husbands, fathers, and sweethearts who had just sailed back into port, or to bid farewell to those who were leaving.

The excitement she had felt earlier Priscilla at first believed to be her own, hers and that of the other seven girls clustered together as they walked along the uneven surface of the streets. Now she realized it belonged to all of Portsmouth, to the Province, perhaps, since this was the port for New Hampshire and nowadays all roads seemed to lead to the river's mouth and the shipyards and berths and moorings there.

Augusta flushed. "I didn't think," she said. "Just look around. Are there always this many ships in port?"

Priscilla shrugged. She felt as though she was seeing everything for the first time, her senses sharpened and quickened by the importance of the occasion. Just ahead of her marched Helen Seavey, striding along with even steps, her dark-red skirt partly hidden under a plain black cloak. Everyone had followed Helen's lead in the matter of dress. Remembering the struggle she had had with herself over the wearing of her brown wool when she wanted so badly to put on the less ancient green, Priscilla wondered how Mary Langdon had been able to close her eyes to the many pretty gowns in her wardrobe and to wear again the dark-blue she'd had on at the Quilting Party. At that, Priscilla thought resentfully, looking around at the others, Mary's dress is far and away the newest and finest here, although it may be an everyday frock to her.

It was the last day of October, one of those crystalline days that are found in autumn along the northeastern coastline. The sky was blue and immense, the sun golden and providing a warmth that Priscilla could feel gratefully on her face. It was cold, though. The east wind that created so much trouble for the Captain swept in from the Isles of Shoals and she was glad of the thickness of her cloak. She wondered if Anna, who grasped tightly at her own threadbare shawl, was warm enough. Instinctively, Priscilla moved ahead and to the right of Anna, hoping to shelter her from as much of the bitter east wind as possible. Anna came closer to Priscilla, her pinched little face twisting into a smile under the flopping brim of her bonnet.

"It's c-crisp, isn't it!" she exclaimed. "But isn't it exciting!"

Not even Anna Hilton would complain today, Priscilla thought. Their mission seemed to paint a golden sheen on everything, as the sunlight gilded masts, touched the features of carved figureheads, washed over idly flapping canvas drying in the fresh clear air, caressed plumes and bonnets. Priscilla sighed happily and marched along with the others, enjoying her awareness of the flag folded on Helen's outstretched hands and straining constantly for her first glimpse of the *Ranger*.

The eight girls had met, at Helen's request if not her command, in front of Mr. Fowle's little printing office on Pleasant Street.

"Mr. Fowle helped me so much, at the outset," Helen had explained, "that I think he should see the result. To be truthful, girls," she added, "it was he who told me Captain Paul Jones had expressed his desire for a flag. So the idea was really his, not mine."

"You carried it out," Augusta had said loyally. "Daniel Fowle could not sew a flag. Nor give his wedding dress up to make it from, either!"

Helen had been waiting just inside the shop. When she saw the others hurrying along the street, she had come out at once. Her face was shining with pride and happiness, and Priscilla knew that the eyes of Mr. Fowle, the first to see it besides themselves, Dorothy's aunt, and doubtless Helen's mother, had found the new flag acceptable.

"Did he like it?" "What did he say?" "Did he think we'd got it right, Helen?" they clamored, and Helen first nodded hard and then shook her head, to show them she was too much moved at the moment to tell them now what had been said behind the wooden door. Glancing backward at the dingy window, Priscilla saw the round balding head of the peppery little publisher of the *Gazette* as he peered after them. He was wiping first the glasses in his hand and then his eyes, and she know well enough what he thought of their gift.

Their walk, which sometimes took on the semblance of a march, Priscilla thought as she hurried along, led them down Pleasant Street and then by the meetinghouse to the waterfront. There, for some reason, Helen took an indirect route. They went past Lears' and the long rope walk nearby, turned left on Mechanic Street, and passed the fine hip-roofed mansion built by Madam Mark Hunking Wentworth, great-aunt to Priscilla, for her son Thomas as a wedding gift. This house, overshadowed by a huge linden tree brought all the way from England seventeen years before, was Betsy's favorite of all the houses in Portsmouth. Priscilla knew that she dreamed of herself and Daniel Wendell living in just such a house.

The group hurried by the little Point of Graves burying ground and passed the Liberty Pole, erected in 1766, with its flatly stated inscription: "Liberty, property, and no stamps." There, just ahead, was Jacob Sheafe's warehouse where the sloop was lying. Priscilla thought how different a ship looked when it was fully fitted and nearly ready to sail. White canvas was rolled and lashed in place. Myriad ropes crisscrossed to make a pattern with the three tall masts and the many horizontal yards. The black paint on her hull was bright, and the gilded scrolls along the bow gleamed in the sun, as did the yellow figurehead and the broad yellow stripe with its nine square gunports. The cluttered deck was a scene of great activity, as men rolled barrels along its length or hurried up gangplanks bearing great burdens, every small antlike figure intent on completing one duty in order to begin another.

As they reached the side of the *Ranger*, Helen spoke quickly to one of the men standing by the gangplank. He gave her a grin, motioned for them to wait, and went aboard the sloop. When he returned, still without saying a word, he beckoned the girls aboard. Helen carried her burden, wrapped in a length of clean linen, as though she were a high priestess. Priscilla, picking her way carefully up the tilted boarding plank, felt her heart pounding unbearably. From their silence she knew the other girls must feel the same way. If they were not excited almost to the point of fainting, they would be chittering and chirping as they stepped on the deck.

The group huddled together where their taciturn guide had led them, in the shelter of a pile of crates. Priscilla glanced up at the sky, saw the masts incredibly far above her, and looked away quickly.

"It makes you dizzy to see them, doesn't it?" murmured Mary, who was standing next to her. "Fancy how it would be if one was at sea, and the ship rolling!"

"Don't!" giggled Caroline. "It makes me want to run to the rail, just to think of it." Augusta emitted a shrill, nervous cackle which she stifled abruptly.

Priscilla had experienced the dizziness too and decided to look in other directions. She half turned so that she could see the harbor. It seemed to be filled with small craft. Dories from the vessels at anchor were plying back and forth between ships and shore. Fishing boats were coming in, many with baskets of gleaming silver fish to sell to the ships' cooks who leaned over rails to bargain for the catch. Everywhere were the Piscataqua gundalows, with their stumpy masts, designed to carry passengers and freight up the river and under its many bridges. To Priscilla and the others the gundalows were so familiar as to be hardly noticeable, but she had been told that nowhere else in this country could these serviceable little craft be found, although it was said they had been copied after boats in Italy or some other European country.

Across the river, on Langdon's Island, more antlike figures were working on new ships. One, she saw, was being readied for launching, poised above the slanting incline down which it would slide to become another privateer to prey upon the enemy. Two were mere skeletons, and from this distance appeared so small and flimsy one wondered how they could ever carry men and goods and sail great distances on the wild, open sea.

Just leaving Long Wharf, with men tugging at the ropes to unfurl the sails, was a ship that Priscilla had never seen before. She wondered what its name was, who owned it, which of the people she knew in Portsmouth would be sailing on this voyage. I must have been unconscious all my life! she thought with amazement. There is nothing more exciting than a ship leaving for foreign ports, for fighting at sea, for carrying away lumber and spars, oil and cattle, and bringing back spices and silks and all the pretty things people have in their houses here. Now, she thought, the cargoes wouldn't be so interesting, but the ships themselves were romantic and exciting. She had been too wrapped up in herself and in her little life to heed them. All that, she promised herself, would be changed.

There was a stirring beside her, murmurs, sighs. She turned quickly. Her heart gave a great leap when she saw the figure approaching. Captain Jones was impeccably groomed, as always, looking like an outsider among the working, disheveled men. Yet as he walked toward them he spoke to first one and then another, giving orders or directions, making suggestions, bestowing bits of praise, showing clearly to the waiting girls that his finger was in every pie and nothing was going on aboard his ship with which he was not totally familiar.

Priscilla had seen him in his dress uniform many times, but here, with the sun glinting on his gold buttons and single gold epaulet and on the gold lace edging his white waistcoat and dark-blue coat, with his gleaming white breeches and stockings, he seemed the most elegant and handsome figure in the world.

"Young ladies." He stood before them, removing his plumed hat with its jaunty black cockade. The sun glossed his dark hair, and the fresh breeze stirred it. "I am honored to have you aboard my ship today. I wish that I could show it to you, all of it, but as you see it is impossible to walk about. It is even dangerous to stand still, I think, but we will chance it for a little while."

"Captain Jones." Helen's voice, usually so strong and sure, seemed to falter. Priscilla looked at her in astonishment. She would not have believed that Helen Seavey could be made nervous by anything in the world. Yet she stood there, her face white under her dark bonnet, her voice higher and less strong than usual. "Captain Jones, we have—brought you something. Something we hope that you will like. We—it—it is the best we could do, sir, and we—we hope that it is all right."

She thrust forward the flat bundle she had been carrying all this time. "Oh," she cried nervously. "No, not this. Just—" Her fingers fumbled with the linen wrapped around the flag, but it was Mary Langdon who leaned over and deftly twitched the linen off, revealing the silken red and white stripes, and a bit of the dark-blue field.

Priscilla felt a lump in her throat. She swallowed, but the lump seemed to grow until she wondered if she would disgrace herself by choking. She looked at Betsy's profile and knew that she was suffering in the same way.

She looked at the Captain. His dark eyes were brilliant as he looked from the flag to Helen and slowly around the circle. For a moment he did not speak, but stood there in silence, holding the soft shining silk in his hands.

"Young ladies," he said at last, and Priscilla thought she detected just the slightest quaver in his voice, "you have made me the envy of every ship's commander in the world." Slowly he unfolded the flag, handing a corner to Priscilla, another to Augusta. His own fingers were on the blue field and the lowest stripe. Held above the deck, the silk shimmered and glowed.

"I thank you from the bottom of my heart," he went on. "The *Ranger* will wear your gift proudly, and I promise that she will never disgrace it. Nor will she ever strike her flag, nor allow it to be conquered, I also promise you that. This gift is made not only to me and to the *Ranger* and her men, but it is also made to our country. The nation will hear of it and thank you, as I do."

He turned and spoke to two men standing nearby. "Prepare to fly our flag when we sail tomorrow, on the tide," he said to them in his ringing voice. The men stepped forward and took the flag from him, Priscilla and Augusta relinquishing their hold with reluctance. The men, Priscilla noted, were big rough-looking seamen in torn and dirty clothes. Their hands were dirty too, but they took the flag reverently.

"I wish," the Captain said, "I could ask you to stay

aboard a while, but that I cannot do. In the next few hours we must cram this ship full of all those goods upon the wharf. We would prefer to have three or four days to perform this task, but since we have so little time—"

"Come on, girls." Helen's voice, Priscilla noted with amusement, had become strong again. "A pleasant voyage to you, Captain. We will remove ourselves from everyone's path."

"A pleasant voyage!" fussed Dorothy as she seized Priscilla's arm to help herself down the plank. "You'd think the man was going for an afternoon sail around the Isles of Shoals, instead of into a war and all the way to France. A pleasant voyage."

Priscilla was about to chide her friend for criticizing Helen at such a moment, but she realized that Dorothy too was acting under the strain of emotion. Priscilla herself felt drained dry and so exhausted she wondered if she would be able to manage the long walk home. Just as her feet stepped down carefully on the rough planks of the wharf, she heard her name called.

"Mark!" she cried.

"So you did come to see me off."

"Of course." She crossed her fingers under her cloak. She wouldn't, for anything in the world, have Mark Jaffrey know that she had scarcely given him a thought, before this moment.

"I saw your flag," he said easily. "I was just above your head on the mainmast when the Captain unfurled it. It is a brave flag indeed, and a fine piece of work. Did you realize it may be the very first one for the colonies, Priscilla? At least I heard that Mr. Fowle, down at the paper, said one was being made here and he thought it would be the very first."

"Yes, we knew. Or at least, we hoped. It was all Helen Seavey's idea," Priscilla said. "Hers, and Mr. Fowle's."

"And you helped to make it," Mark said. "Every time I look at it, I will think of you, Priscilla. Not that I need some colored silk to remind me of you."

She smiled up at him. How soft his eyes were, almost like brown velvet, like that cape of Sarah Wendell's that Betsy so admires! He too was wearing a uniform, with a dark-blue coat and white breeches, but he had no gold epaulet or lace, and his coat lacked white lapels. His head was bare, and his hair, thick and soft, was gilded in the sun. He was no longer that too-tall, too-thin boy she remembered, but a man grown and a handsome one at that, especially in his trim new uniform.

Mark saw her eyes fall to his attire and said, "Did you not know I sail with Captain Jones as one of his midshipmen, Priscilla?"

"But, Mark, that is fine!" she exclaimed, thinking to herself, Wait until I tell Betsy about this. She put on such airs over Daniel's being a midshipman. Of course she says Daniel will be made a lieutenant at once, since his father wishes him to be, but just the same—"I did not know."

"And you are surprised," he said, laughing at her. "Well, to be truthful with you, I am surprised myself. There are few such berths, you see, and it hadn't occurred to me I might be lucky enough to have one of them. Mr. Livermore, I feel sure, put in a word for me with the Captain, or with Colonel Langdon, who apparently had most to say about the officers. I will learn more of what seamanship is all about, and fighting too, I suppose. I may even have an opportunity to advance. When I come back—*if* I come back—this training will be useful to me."

"Oh, Mark, don't say that!" For some reason Priscilla

was never more aware of Mark's loneliness. He had said "*if* I come back" with a shrug, as much to say he wasn't sure he cared, and he was more than sure that no one else would care. "Of course you will come back, Mark Jaffrey."

"Well then, if you say so." He smiled at her gently. "I won't ask you if I'll find you waiting on the dock when I sail back into the harbor," he told her. "But I have already asked if I may write to you, and you have told me yes. That is enough for now. I must go back and do my duty or I'll find myself not only not a midshipman, but not so much as a sailor aboard the *Ranger*. You will be here in the morning?"

She nodded wordlessly. Mark seized her hand in an unexpected move, squeezed it hard, and with one last brilliant smile, left her, running up the gangplank and disappearing at once from sight. Priscilla, gazing after him, nursed her sore fingers and caught, for just a moment, the dark eyes of the Captain upon her. He smiled at her too, the same knowing smile he had given her in the kitchen the night before. Oh, dear, she thought, now he's *sure* he's right about Mark. And he isn't, he's all wrong. . . .

She turned away. The ship would sail, she knew, at nine tomorrow just after the tide reached its full height. She searched the wharf and at last found Betsy, standing forlornly by herself, her gray eyes brimming with tears.

"I've just said good-by to Daniel," she whispered to Priscilla. "Perhaps forever. Who knows? I could die, right here, and I wish I would. Oh, Pris, why do things have to be this way?"

Chapter 8

SOMETHING TO DO

W̲E̲ HAVE SHIPS sailing from this harbor every day," Priscilla said later. "Almost, anyway. Why was that one so —so—you know?"

Priscilla, with her mother and Betsy, was busy turning out the room that the Captain had occupied for so many weeks. The surroundings brought back to Priscilla the day when the *Ranger* had left nearly two months before. As predicted, the wind had changed and had blown crisp and strong from the White Mountains and down the Piscataqua. She remembered the deep boom of the gun, fifes piping and drums tapping smartly as the men turned the capstan to break out the anchor, white sails filling as the sloop of war turned in the channel and headed for sea. She remembered voices raised in cheers and loud cries, tears running down cheeks, shouts from shore and from other ships in the harbor, small craft stopped all over the surface of the water, men resting on their oars and waving their caps to the *Ranger*. And she remembered the flag fluttering high above the stern, looking smaller and smaller as the *Ranger* moved rapidly away.

"Why was it so tearful and noisy, at the same time?"

Mrs. Purcell, her chestnut-brown hair tucked up under a kerchief, was washing the white-painted windowsills with rapid, deft motions. At first she had told her two older daughters that perhaps they could move down from their third-floor room and occupy this one. Priscilla had been thrilled at the thought of waking up in the morning to look at the same windows the Captain had seen first every day, the same tree branches, the same chairs and table, Mrs. Purcell had delayed her decision week after week. Finally a Mr. St. John of Boston had inquired at the door, sent to Mrs. Purcell by Mr. Langdon, who knew that the newcomer did not want to stay at Stoodley's or the Earl of Rockingham or the William Pitt, but preferred a large room in a quiet house. Reluctantly, Priscilla had given up her dream of living where the Captain had lived, walking each day on boards where his feet had so lately stepped.

"It's just as well," Betsy said cheerfully. "I hate living up in the attic with Jerusha and Molly—after all, I *am* Miss Purcell, the eldest daughter of the house—but if we had the big corner room, in no time at all Mother would put Meggie and Susan in the little room next, for us to look after, and Sarah and Mary and Hannah would have a room of their own as large as ours and no children to care for."

Priscilla had shaken her head. Ever since Daniel Wendell had sailed away with the Captain, Betsy had seemed to turn inward. The slightest detail of her daily life now became of the greatest importance to her. The petty disputes and rivalries between the sisters, which had never touched Betsy before, so wrapped up in Daniel had she been, now assumed great proportions. She was as contentious and sulky about her rights and privileges as small Sarah, who was forever demanding equal favors with Mary, although Mary was two years older.

Priscilla's heart wasn't in her cleaning chore, because

she was performing it for an unknown Mr. St. John, but she took some small pleasure in dusting surfaces where the Captain's fingers might have rested and dresser drawers where his fine white shirts and neatly folded neckerchiefs had been. Her mind went back to the day, the first day of November, when the *Ranger* had left the harbor. Two whole months ago, two months while her mother had tried to make up her mind about renting the room again, two months without word from the *Ranger,* except for a ship or two that had come to port having met her at sea, not far away.

"I think," Mrs. Purcell said carefully, "that each sailing has much the same combination of gloom and holiday excitement attending it. But that one, Priscilla, happened to mean something to you personally. So you noticed it more."

"I've been down at the harbor and watched many of them sail," Priscilla said shortly. "Even the *Raleigh*—and we were all so proud of her, the first ship built here for the navy. People waved and shouted then, and I suppose some of the women cried, but I didn't happen to see them. No, Mother, it was different with the *Ranger.* Betsy, don't you think I'm right?"

Betsy's gray eyes were filmed with familiar tears, and Priscilla wondered angrily why she had been foolish enough to recall Betsy's sorrow. Most of the time Daniel was not mentioned in the house. Betsy obviously made a great effort to forget about her personal loss, but now Priscilla had forgotten and brought up the taboo subject herself.

"I wouldn't know," Betsy said crossly. "I was one of those weeping women, remember?"

Mrs. Purcell, glancing quickly at her oldest daughter, sat down to rest in a straight-backed chair.

"I believe what I said is true, Priscilla," she said in her

calm, even voice. "You were more aware of what was being said and felt because you yourself were concerned. We knew the Captain, we all did, and that could have made the difference. But truthfully, I believe your senses were sharpened by the fact that you, yourself, were a part of that scene."

"You mean by being there? But I've been there before, and I—"

"No, Pris, you silly thing, she doesn't mean that. I know what you're trying to say, Mother, and I think you're right. We were there for a special reason, Pris. Not just to wave good-by to Daniel and Mark and the Captain and the others. We—well, in a way we were part of the ship itself. The flag—oh, how tiny it looked at the end, didn't it? No bigger than the stitches we took in it, really! But we had sewed ourselves into that flag, in a way. I don't mean just Helen's wedding dress, or Mary's beautiful red ball gown, or Augusta's China-silk petticoat and our own scraps, but ourselves. Our prayers, I suppose. Our thoughts. Little bits of —of us. So the flag and the ship meant something extra to us, and—well, don't you think perhaps the flag had much to do with all the emotion and excitement?"

"Yes, dear, I do. That is precisely what I was trying to say." Mrs. Purcell stood up and put her palms to the small of her back wearily. "Oh, dear, I am tired. Can you girls finish up here, do you think? We are having two extra guests at dinner today, and I have forgotten to tell Caddie about them."

"Go ahead, Mother, we'll finish. There isn't much more to do." Priscilla fluttered her cloth at her mother with a shooing motion. "Mother seems awfully tired lately," she said with concern as they heard Mrs. Purcell's footsteps descend slowly. "Don't you think, Betsy?"

Betsy rubbed hard at the surface of the gateleg table she was polishing. "Yes, I do, Pris. Maybe we could somehow take on a little more of the work, you and I. I do think Hannah could help. She isn't needed every minute to stay with the children, she just happens to like it. Let's get her to working with us. Pris, do you have the feeling that you'd like to work yourself to the bone, to get so tired every day that you just drop into bed at night, so that you go to sleep right away and wouldn't dream, even? Do you?"

"Why, no, Betsy. Do you?" Suddenly, Priscilla realized that Betsy had been working unusually hard lately. "Do you, really?"

"Yes." Betsy put the table back under the window where it belonged and surveyed the room critically. "Aren't we about done now, Pris? I don't think Jerusha did a very good job on the floor, but it's too late to correct that. It'll have to stay that way. Yes, I have this feeling of wanting simply to exhaust myself every day. I dread going to bed. I used to lie there and have the most beautiful daydreams! In fact I couldn't wait to go to bed at night, so I could think about D-daniel and the future and how wonderful it would be. But now—" She turned and looked out of the window, her back stiff and despairing. "Now—I can't stand it. Perhaps there isn't any future. Daniel may never come back. That's all I can think of, Pris. Don't you feel the same way about Mark? Tell me the truth."

Priscilla shook her head. "Betsy Purcell, I hardly know Mark, and you know it. So how could I feel anything about him, one way or the other?"

Betsy threw her sister an angry look. "Oh, you always were much too closemouthed," she said crossly. "I don't see why we can't be friends." She flounced out through the door. Priscilla heard her running up the stairs to their own room, where no doubt she would throw herself on the bed and indulge in one of her crying spells.

Priscilla crossed to the window and looked out at the dead garden which was, unlike most Portsmouth gardens, in front of the house. In summer the sunken, terraced space bloomed with roses and snapdragons, which gave way to asters and chrysanthemums, but now at the very end of the year it was bleak and deserted, with a few clumps of dried yellow grasses and stems in even rows. She ran her finger over the name the Captain had scratched on one window and put her forehead against the cool glass, wondering if he had often stood in this spot, enjoying the colorful display below.

And what do I think of Mark? she asked herself, again not for the first time. He had been a gawky, shy boy, and he was now a fairly handsome young man. He must have considerable merit, or the Captain would not have signed him on as midshipman, since presumably he has had no experience on ships. But neither has Daniel Wendell or the other one either, and how about that Lieutenant Wallingford? Is it a matter of education? Daniel has had schooling, but surely Mark hasn't, except for the little Colonel Whipple and Mr. Livermore have given him. Still, that probably does count. Perhaps the Captain chose Mark for the same reason that Mr. Livermore selected him, because he sees something special in him, something worth bothering with and educating.

Poor Mark, her mind went on. His mother isn't interested in him, and he has no one else. And he asked if he could write me. But I must write him! she thought, wondering why such a simple idea had not crossed her mind before. That is what he wanted, that was what he was asking for. Betsy has been writing long letters to Daniel ever since the *Ranger* sailed. I will write to him right now and ask her how to send it. When they give out mail in some port, Mark Jaffrey won't be the only one who doesn't receive anything from home.

The letter was not easy to write. She knew almost nothing about Mark, so she had little idea what would interest him. She told him about the six men who were now regular boarders at the Purcells', of the unknown Mr. St. John who would soon live in the Captain's room. She told him the story that was all over town about the man who had bought a few pounds of wool, and how Mr. Sheafe had, in a mirror, happened to see him slip a small cheese into the sack. Mr. Sheafe had then insisted that he had mis-weighed the wool and that the bag must be put on the scales again, although the man had protested. The purchase had, of course, weighed a great deal more than before, and the unfortunate and dishonest customer had paid in dollars for a cheese that would have cost him only a few cents.

Mark will enjoy that story because he said he had worked for a short time for Jacob Sheafe. Probably every other letter on board will tell the same tale, but what else is there to say?

When she had finished, Priscilla only half admitted to herself that she was in truth writing a letter to the Captain. He knew Sheafe's well. He would be interested in the new boarders. He would perhaps be sorry to learn that his room was about to be taken over by another. But whether she was writing to Mark or to the Captain, Priscilla acknowledged that she had nothing to say. Nothing about herself. Nothing happens to me, she thought angrily. What could I write down of interest to anyone? That I got up in the morning and scrubbed my face and had breakfast and spent the morning washing paint and window glass? That when Caddie burned her hand on the brick oven, I helped bandage it for her? That Sunday I caught my best skirt in the door of the counting room and made a tear six inches long?

I ought to *do* something, she thought. Then I shall have something to write the Captain about. Not the Captain, Mark, she reproved herself sternly. But I really must do something worth writing about in a letter.

For the next few days Priscilla went around in a daze. She didn't hear people when they spoke to her, forgot to perform errands she had been given, and neglected her daily chores. She was trying, all the time and as hard as she could, to think of something she could *do*. A part of a remark, overheard as she was serving at the dinner table one noon, gave her her first clue.

"In a city as widely split in allegiance as this one, a certain amount of spying and smuggling is bound to go on."

The speaker was pompous little Mr. Jonathan Evans. He had been a steady boarder ever since Sarah Purcell had decided to conduct her "genteel" boardinghouse. Although he had seldom uttered a word when the Captain was present, he had elected himself chief spokesman since, and at the moment was fussily trying to explain everything about Portsmouth to the newcomer, Mr. St. John.

"You see, sir," Mr. Evans went on, "this town is, or at least was before the trouble began, one of the wealthiest on the seaboard. The West Indian trade was thriving here, before blockades and privateering became the order of the day. Just look about you, sir, at the imposing mansions built with money derived from building ships, or sailing them, or selling their cargoes. Not so ornate, I grant you, as those in Salem, but with a certain remarkable beauty all their own, and all extremely well built. I know building, sir—I have been in the lumber business all my life, and my father was a fine cabinetmaker, none better, and I tell you that the workmanship and artistry that has gone into the construction of many Portsmouth homes is without equal."

"You were speaking," Mr. St. John ventured mildly, "of the divided allegiance in this city." Mr. St. John was a slim man of medium height, and he was, Priscilla thought, all gray. Gray hair, gray eyes behind rimmed spectacles, drab gray garments. She hurried to the pantry to get the gravy for the chicken and wondered why Mr. St. John continued to ask questions. He should know, she thought as she carefully picked up the heavy gravy boat, that he'll only get more talk from that stupid little man.

She had missed some of the answer. Mr. Evans was now saying, "Possibly because it was the seat of the Royal Provincial government. So many families had made so much money in trade and shipping, and they formed a sort of aristocracy here. They ringed themselves around the Royal Family, so to speak, I mean the Wentworths, sir, of course." Throwing an apprehensive look toward the empty chair where Mrs. Purcell sat when she dined with her guests, he added, in a sort of whisper, "Our gracious hostess is, you understand, a Wentworth. Cousin—first cousin, I believe—to the John Wentworth who was the last Royal Governor, and oddly enough, also to the other John Wentworth who became the first Governor after New Hampshire declared itself an independent colony. You cannot go far in Portsmouth, sir, without running into a Wentworth, let me tell you. John Wentworth who was, back in 1717, Lieutenant Governor here, had something like sixteen children. Most of whom grew up and were married and had children of their own. Mark Hunking Wentworth, the first

John's son, was father to the second John, who was, as I said before, our last Royal Governor."

"And the divided allegiance?" Mr. St. John pursued politely.

"Ah. Well, you see, sir, with this layer of aristocracy in the town, we had, you might say, a fairly cohesive band of Tories, ready-made and waiting for the conflict. No question of which side most would be on—they were too close to the Wentworths and to the Crown. When Governor John and his lady sailed back to England, a few of them, for one reason or another, switched over to uphold the new government. But many did not. There was even division in the Wentworth family itself. Governor John's own father and several of his uncles have been true and active patriots, you know, all along. Our gracious Mrs. Purcell's father among them, of course. Still, since the Independence a goodly number have left us. You must have encountered many of our former citizens in Boston, sir, since you have lived there for some time. Some have gone to Halifax, or elsewhere in Nova Scotia where their loyalties will be approved by their neighbors. Some have returned to England. But many are living here, quite peaceably, at least on the surface. For one thing, privateering and the profits therefrom are attractive to all, no matter with which flag one's sympathies may lie. But if you stop to think on it, underneath the calm exterior there must be plots and counterplots, there must be tempers that simmer and even boil. After all, these men have a cause, even as you and I. A cause they believe in—again, even as you and I. And why would they not do what they could to help out that cause? There has been some loose talk going about recently of an attempt to seize such stores of ammunition and arms as may be found around here. That, sir, could be named robbery!"

Mr. St. John looked mildly around at the silent faces and back to Mr. Evans.

"But," he said, "I would be very much surprised if either arms or ammunition could be found in this neighborhood. Very much surprised, indeed. On my very first evening here, Mr. Evans, you yourself told me of the removal from your fort of all military stores. You also told me that the ringleader, along with Major Sullivan, was John Langdon and that his cousin Samuel, whom I have known all my life, took the powder to Cambridge and later to Valley Forge."

"The stores were floated up Great Bay and taken inland," Mr. Evans agreed. "As you say, much of it was delivered at once to our army. But not all. Furthermore, the fort did not hold all the arms and ammunition that existed, you know. There were many such stores, here or there."

By this time Priscilla had cleared the table and served the dessert. She was now standing by the pantry door, unabashedly listening as hard as she could.

The next voice surprised her.

"I must tell you," said the soft whisper of little Mr. Mason, "that I was present when our men tried to force Jonathan Warner, then commissary, to give up the keys to his storehouse. He refused, quite properly too, since his was a trusted position, so to speak. But do you know, Mr. St. John, what he said to the Sons of Liberty? He said, 'If you break in my door, gentlemen, what can I do?' So of course they did so, and the very next day he said to one of them, a particular friend of mine, 'You know, the Sons of Liberty broke into my storehouse last night. I should not be surprised if they do it again tonight.' All of his storehouse was well emptied after that, I can tell you!"

Mr. Evans sounded, Priscilla thought, a trifle annoyed at the interruption, for he went on quickly.

"I have often thought that some of our waterfront warehouses, for example, could bear watching at the moment. Several are owned by known Tories. What could be simpler than to smuggle a few guns or barrels of powder into a warehouse, to be loaded in the dark of night into a gundalow or fishing boat and rowed away? It would not be a large amount, but, let us say, a steady trickle which could add up in time to a sizeable theft of our stores. However, Mr. St. John, as I said before, in a city where allegiances are split and every man a patriot to his own cause, a great deal must be going on at night when no one is looking. Spies must be lurking in our city, men who come in in crews of ships and drop ashore to stay and do their deadly work against us."

Priscilla peered around the door in time to see Mr. Tilton look down at Mr. Evans coldly. Mr. Tilton was an extremely tall man, with a long beak of a nose that always seemed to be disapproving. Mr. Mason and Mr. Evans, on either side of him at the table, were unusually short, which made Mr. Tilton seem even taller than he was.

"I believe, Mr. Evans, that possibly we are borrowing trouble this day," he said. "Perhaps if we all returned to the work we are supposed to be doing, we will have less time for such idle and speculative talk."

The men scraped back their chairs without a word. Mr. Tilton certainly put an end to that conversation, Priscilla thought with a chuckle. But her mind was busy with the words Mr. Evans had spoken before Mr. Tilton stopped him.

Spies, she thought. Smugglers. Here in Portsmouth! Maybe I could catch one! I could be a heroine all by myself. Then I would have something to write about to the Captain—I mean, to Mark!

Chapter 9

A TIMID STEP

FROM THE FIRST of the year Priscilla searched for her spy. It was one problem to catch a spy once you knew there was one, but she was finding it difficult indeed to discover anyone who appeared in the least suspicious and worth chasing.

Her first candidate was Mr. St. John. "He came here so mysteriously," she explained to Dorothy one snowy afternoon in January. "Just appeared at the door wanting a room."

"Oh la, Priscilla Purcell," Dorothy grinned at her. "Everyone is mysterious until you find out that he is not! I mean, the town is full of strangers, and they cannot all be spies. Most are simply men from Salem or Boston or Newburyport or other places going about their business."

From the beginning, Dorothy refused to take Priscilla's notion seriously. Priscilla often wondered why she had confided in her friend at all, except that she distinctly felt the need of some help with her plans.

"But he kept on and on at Mr. Evans," Priscilla explained. "Every time he got off the road in his conversation—you know he never stops talking and sometimes gets all tangled up. But whenever he wandered, Mr. St. John gave him that fishy glance and urged him back to the subject of divided loyalty and all that."

"Mr. St. John no doubt has an inquiring mind," Dorothy said, yawning. "Like my Uncle Elijah. Just last night Colonel James was talking to my aunt about him. He said, 'Elizabeth, not only is your husband a man of many talents, but he has one of the greatest gifts a man can have, an inquiring mind.' "

Priscilla giggled. "What was she going on about this time?" she asked. Ever since the sailing of the *Ranger*, with Dorothy's Uncle Elijah, Mrs. Hall had made life miserable for her household with a constant stream of complaints.

"Why hadn't he written? Why hadn't we heard? Why hadn't he been content to stay at Langdon's and build more ships instead of sailing away? You know, one thing leads to another. Colonel James told her that no one had heard a word yet, that it was too soon, that even the Captain had said the voyage over would take a month, and so on."

Priscilla's spy was completely forgotten for the moment. "I know," she said sadly, "I wish we would hear."

This was early January. Within the next fortnight letters from the men on the *Ranger* did come in on a battle-scarred British frigate taken by an American ship and sailed into Portsmouth under a prize crew. Every recipient of a letter appreciated the miracle. The letters had been transferred from captor to the captured ship and had survived not only the fierce battle, but the transfer. Sacks of mail were thrown from deck to wharf by the weary crew. The contents of the letters were devoured, and the creased, thumbmarked papers had passed from hand to hand. Most of the letters, long or short, spoke of the trip over. The

Captain had crowded sail on his ship and driven the *Ranger* hard in order to deliver his message to the Americans waiting for it in France. Dorothy's uncle wrote at great length to his father-in-law, Colonel Stoodley. Although he had the greatest respect for the Captain's seamanship, the way he drove his ship through snow squalls and black, starless nights, and through days of biting cold when men who stayed on deck too long well might freeze to death, was reported a frightening experience for them all.

It appeared from the letters that the Captain had chosen a fast course rather than a pleasant one. "Imagine, then," wrote Dorothy's uncle, "the situation of the *Ranger*'s crew, with a top-heavy and crank ship under their feet and a commander who day and night insisted on every rag she could stagger under without laying clear down!"

Dorothy and Priscilla shivered over that together. Not even Dorothy seemed worried by the fact that the Captain had risked the neck of her uncle, among others, to gain time. But they were upset to learn that, after all the strain and stress of the harrowing voyage, Captain Jones was not the first to place in the hands of Dr. Benjamin Franklin the news of Burgoyne's surrender. The day before his arrival on December 5, a Mr. Austin of Boston had reached Passy, outside of Paris, and handed duplicate dispatches to the American commissioners.

"He must have been so disappointed," the girls mourned. "He loves to be first at everything. And he tried so hard to get there first!"

A trifle uneasily, they noticed that Lieutenant Elijah Hall no longer seemed a great admirer of the Captain. They sensed from his letter that he had somehow cooled, although it was difficult to believe. Time and time again Priscilla sought reassurance between the lines of her own brief letter from Mark. He too had spoken of the fearful voyage over, but instead of dwelling on the dangers and the hardships, he had written glowingly of the Captain's genius for sailing. He wrote that the Captain was never above giving a hand at any task, however menial or uncomfortable.

Priscilla, to her own surprise, was a trifle disappointed that Mark had not added a personal message beyond a polite, "I trust this finds you well, and your family. Please give my kind regards to your mother." Mark and her mother had little more than a nodding acquaintance. He might have sent his regards to Priscilla herself, she thought, but she said nothing. Betsy had received a letter from Daniel that had quite evidently exceeded all of her expectations. She went around with her eyes shining and the letter rustling inside her bodice where she could take it out and read and reread it to her heart's content. The very fact that her sister allowed no one to look at the precious paper told Priscilla that Daniel had at last discovered within himself some affection for Betsy Purcell.

Priscilla and Dorothy avidly read every letter they could get their hands on, hoping for additional crumbs of information about their captain. The least pleasant words they discarded—complaints, doubts, veiled hints that threatened of rebellion. Priscilla even managed to forget the letter written by the Captain himself to John Wendell, in which he praised Daniel as a "promising and deserving young man"—which, of course, transported Betsy into new heights—and mentioned "the fair Miss Wendell."

"Of course he *had* to say that, to be polite," Priscilla told Dorothy haughtily. "After all, Sarah Wendell plays hostess for her father. It is merely good manners to speak of her."

In the next batch of mail the girls learned that their idol

was to remain in France for an indefinite period.

"But I thought he would come right back!" Dorothy wailed. "After all, he only had to deliver a message. He should come home now."

It appeared that negotiations and intrigues were going on behind closed doors. As Dorothy said sharply, "The Captain, since he speaks absolutely perfect French, will be needed." Neither Dorothy nor Priscilla could imagine anything important taking place without the presence of the Captain. What he actually stayed for, they learned later, was to take command of a new ship being built in Amsterdam and called *L'Indien*.

"Our flag flying on *L'Indien*! On a ship built in Holland!" they marveled. "How exciting!" Dorothy quickly arranged a tea party at the tavern, inviting all the members of their Quilting Party to discuss this fascinating new development.

"The flag should stay with the *Ranger*," Betsy argued. Daniel had written Betsy that some of the men were leaving the *Ranger* with the Captain, but that he and Lieutenant Hall and many others planned to remain on their ship and serve under Lieutenant Simpson.

"There will be other flags," Helen said calmly. "But ours —the very first of all—was made for Captain Paul Jones. It must go where he goes."

"Oh, how dull it is!" exclaimed Mary Langdon. Although her remark had nothing to do with the subject at hand, the girls understood. There seemed to be no men around these days. Helen herself looked grave, because she had not heard from her husband for too long, and Caroline's fiancé had been wounded.

"My party wasn't much of a success, was it?" Dorothy mourned afterward. "I thought it would cheer us up so.

Oh, dear, if only we could have some good news for a change!"

When they argued about the changing of the flag from the *Ranger* to *L'Indien,* the girls had, as it turned out, wasted their breath. The next messages reported that Captain Paul Jones wasn't to have command of *L'Indien* anyway. Priscilla heard of this before any of them. For some reason Betsy had no letter from Daniel in the pouch of letters thrown off the packet onto the boards of Long Wharf, while Dorothy's uncle had written to his wife that he thought that he would soon be returning to America on the *Ranger* under Lieutenant Simpson, with "the great Captain going on to greater glory," he had added irritably.

But Priscilla had a long letter from Mark from a place called Paimboeuf. "The Captain is in Paris, with the swells," he wrote. "And we are here doing what must be done to the *Ranger,* shortening the mainmast and stepping it aft a bit, scraping the hull—in other words, carrying out his instructions. We're having new sails made, too, since those supplied were inferior stuff. The men don't like it here—there's nothing to do but work, which does not please them, and besides, they want to be at sea where they can take prizes and make money. I do not complain. I am busy, I am in France, and I have my own thoughts. It is cold, which I had not expected. Snow, once in a while, and there is ice floating down the Loire. This too makes the men grumble, and they point out they were promised 'an agreeable voyage in a pleasant season.' The voyage was far from agreeable and the season is fair unpleasant. There is a great deal of complaint against Captain Jones, which I suppose is to be expected. It appears to be human nature to dislike whoever is in charge and gives the orders. We have just heard—a few minutes ago actually, after I began this letter to you—that he is returning to us after all. There will be more grumbling now, I'm afraid. Most of this criticism of the Captain comes from Thomas Simpson, who, as you know, is Mr. Langdon's brother-in-law. He and the Captain have disliked each other from the start, and for some reason we feel constrained to choose up sides, a situation that should not exist."

Priscilla wondered vaguely if people back home would find themselves "choosing up sides." She hoped not. Mary Langdon would naturally feel loyalty to her uncle. Dorothy's uncle, from the tone of his letters, was lined up against the Captain, so probably Dorothy would be too, unthinkable as that seemed.

Priscilla sighed and agreed with Dorothy's wistful prayer for good news. For once their prayers were answered. A ship sailed into the harbor only a few days after the packet, bearing with it more mail from the men, which was quickly distributed and eagerly read. Some of the local wags remarked that the officers and crew of the *Ranger* were drawing their pay under false pretenses, since they obviously had nothing to do but write letters home.

The latest intelligence was exciting enough to warrant another meeting of the Quilting Party, this time in the spacious parlor of the Langdons' home. Their flag, the flag made of Helen's wedding dress and Mary's best red-silk gown and their own petticoats—had been saluted by the guns of a French fleet.

"The first American flag ever!" Helen exclaimed. "Ever! Anywhere! *Our* flag!"

"Only nine guns," observed Anna, who could find something disparaging to say about almost anything.

"That makes no difference," Caroline protested. "Well, perhaps it did to Captain Paul Jones. But we're only a republic after all."

"What does it *matter!*" Helen cried. "The first American

flag shown on any ocean, and the first to receive and acknowledge a salute from a foreign power. Mr. Fowle told me this was so, and he always knows these things."

"It's just too good to be true," Augusta sighed, her plain features glowing with pride and excitement.

"It is just possible that it is not true," Mary Langdon said carefully. "Oh, gracious, I want it to be true as much as any of you, you know that. But my father said flags on American ships have been saluted before this, certainly once that he knows of, maybe other times."

"Then it was the old Grand Union Flag," Helen maintained stoutly. "Not our flag, the new one. That's not the same thing at all. Of course it's not too good to be true, Augusta. It is what the Captain wanted, and what we most earnestly wanted for it. And for him."

"We should meet each year on the day—that day," Anna Hilton said with unaccustomed spirit and enthusiasm. "And—and celebrate." She flushed as she realized all eyes were on her and looked around apologetically. "I mean—"

"I think that's a splendid idea, Anna," Helen said quickly. "If we're all around next year, and the one after that." She sighed and added briskly, "What was the date, Mary? Of the salute, I mean. The fifteenth?"

Mary unfolded the letter written to her father and searched through the lines on the page. "February fourteenth," she said. "February 14, 1778."

"Then we have an appointment for the fourteenth, next year," Helen said, looking around the circle. "Agreed?"

They were silent going home, setting forth in a little group that broke apart on the way. It was late March. The winds, whistling around them and through the black branches of the bare trees, seemed to penetrate to their bones. Talking would have been difficult in any case, but

Priscilla knew that the others were thinking, as she was, of what must be lived through before the appointment they had just made. Perhaps in that time the *Ranger* would come home, the men would disperse and go back to their families, and the Captain would take up residence again in the corner rooms of the Purcell house, ousting Mr. St. John.

Priscilla had long ago discarded Mr. St. John as a possible spy. He had come to Portsmouth on perfectly legitimate business, and he was close friends with Mr. Langdon and Mr. Wendell and others who would certainly know if there was anything wrong with him. Priscilla had investigated others without any luck.

Dorothy was completely uninterested in uncovering a spy or traitor. She had lately been seeing much of a young man from Salem who, with his uncle, was living at the tavern, and so she shrugged off any suggestion of Priscilla's to pursue the search actively in the town. This threw Priscilla back onto her own resources and ultimately made her more determined than ever to make a name for herself.

In April she began her spy hunt in earnest. The bitter winds of winter were gone. The town was beginning to shake off its cold-weather wrapping and to look forward to spring. The rains had begun and people complained as they did each year, but every day the air became a little warmer, and after each shower the blades of grass seemed to be a trifle longer, a bit greener. Soon buds would appear on the bare limbs of trees. The people were relieved, too, knowing that no longer would men camp in snowdrifts, lose toes and fingers to frostbite, fall from ice-covered spars into the cold, tossing sea.

In Priscilla the weather caused a sort of fever, urging her out of the house, making her want to run about the town, to go somewhere, to do something. "Now," she scolded herself, "you must get on with it, Priscilla Purcell. You have let the winter smother you in heavy clothes and a fear of going out when it is so cold and when it gets dark so early. Now you have no excuse. So, Priscilla Purcell, where will you begin?"

She thought back to the remarks of Mr. Evans, who had to the relief of all of them left Portsmouth and gone south somewhere. They were thoroughly tired of his pompous remarks and his attitudes of great authority on any subject whatsoever. But it was Mr. Evans who had brought the matter up, and he had mentioned the smuggling of guns or powder into warehouses. He had spoken particularly of the waterfront.

"Oh, dear," Priscilla exclaimed. "Why did I not think of the waterfront before? Perhaps I felt down inside that it was too cold to go down to the warehouses. But I no longer have that excuse. So, to work, my girl!"

The next afternoon found her at the waterfront. She first walked the length of Long Wharf, feeling sad because her father's shop had been there. She saw, in a blinding flash, the image of Gregory Purcell striding along the planks, his light hair gleaming, his eyes shining with pleasure at the sight of one or more of his children approaching. Sometimes she seemed to forget her father altogether, to be unable to remember what he looked like. Yet in moments like this one his memory was bright and distinct, and an overwhelming sense of loss swept over her.

So she left Long Wharf, walked past Drifcos and Shapleys' and turned her steps toward Sheafe's warehouse. Jacob Sheafe was a known Tory, although he had not left with the others, nor did he appear to make an issue of it. He simply stayed in Portsmouth, conducting his business as usual and succeeding in minding his own affairs. Perhaps the fact that he was connected in some way with Dorothy Quincy, John Hancock's gay wife, had something to do with it.

But perhaps he is carrying on secretly, she thought. In spite of herself she shivered at the notion. Perhaps he is helping the others smuggle things out by boat. Maybe they use his warehouse, which is so big and dark and always cluttered with all sorts of things that a body'd never know. I'll start there. Mark said—

Priscilla frowned as she hurried along the path that followed the waterfront. How often lately had her thoughts whispered to her, "Mark says. Mark told me. Mark was there." Was it some kind of trick that fate was playing on her, dangling a ghost of Mark Jaffrey in front of her, a trick played on her because Betsy and Dorothy and Helen and Caroline and others had young men to dream about, to worry over, to think of day in and day out? And she, having no one, had appropriated Mark? Or was it because the Captain, being so far away, had dimmed in her mind. She had heard stories about his dancing attention on a duchess, a French *duchesse*, who had given him a watch that belonged to a count, a French naval hero who had been her grandfather. To her he had said that he hoped someday to lay a British frigate at her feet. That sort of tale, Priscilla thought wryly, made him more remote than ever.

So her mind played tricks on her. She was thinking of Mark now as she stepped over rutted cart tracks more deeply carved in mud than ever and reached the warehouse. Sliding inside the door, she saw what appeared to be utter confusion—coiled ropes, lanterns, capstans, piles of canvas, spikes, lengths of wood, planks, a heap of boots, kegs and barrels and boxes. Over it all was a smell of turpentine and kerosine and oil, and of seaweed and the sea.

If Mr. Sheafe asked her what she was doing there, she would say she had been told that Dorothy was to do an errand at the warehouse and she hoped to catch her. But no one seemed to be around. Priscilla picked her way over lengths of rope and around piles of unidentifiable objects in the gloomy interior of the big shed, careful not to fall over something, or to crash into an object that would make a noise. As she crept about stealthily she began to wonder what she was looking for. Since she couldn't name most of the things that she saw, how could she tell what would interest a Tory? Above in the dim light, Priscilla felt her cheeks redden. How stupid, she thought. I'm as bad as a child. Not even Mary or even little Sarah would come into this place without a reason for being here!

She turned and began to pick her way out again, moving with less caution and more speed. Her foot caught the edge of a piece of metal, which slid down a coil of rope and hit a metal lantern on the floor with a crash. Priscilla stopped and held her breath, but there was no sound. Just as she was thankfully about to continue on her way, she heard a footstep, then another. Finally a voice called, "Who's there? Jacob, that you? I've been waiting on you."

Priscilla's hand flew to her throat. It was a man's voice, one she didn't know, and it certainly was not Mr. Sheafe. She saw a glow, heard a clatter from behind, and turned to face a lantern held high. Blinking against the yellow light, she said, "Who—who is it?"

"Who are you? Oh, you're one of the Purcell girls, aren't you? Don't look so scared, miss, it's me, Josiah Whipple. I won't bite, you know. Why are you here?"

"I—I was looking for someone. For my friend, Dorothy Hall," Priscilla said with as much dignity as she could manage. She felt very much at a disadvantage, since he could see her face and she couldn't see his behind the lantern. "I—I guess she's not here. I'll—I'll run along."

"No one here but me," he said cheerfully. "Find your way out all right, can you? Good then. I'll just wait for Jacob. Good-by, Miss Elizabeth or whichever you are."

Chapter 10

A PLAN AT LAST

Betsy, DO YOU remember Josiah Whipple?" Priscilla asked that night as the girls were getting ready for bed.

"Josiah? Joseph, you mean. Or William. And there was a John, I think."

"No, no, not the next-door Whipples, that other family." Priscilla paused with her brush held over her head and looked at Betsy, who was frowning over a torn hem in the skirt she had just taken off.

"I declare, my clothes are in rags," Betsy mourned. "Not that I have anywhere to go to wear decent clothes, but when—"

When Daniel comes home, Priscilla knew she meant. It was true that all their clothes were well worn and inclined to fall apart, and there was never an occasion to wear new dresses, even if one had them. Each Sunday the Purcell girls smoothed and carefully hung their frocks away, remarking that before the war these "Sunday bests" wouldn't have been considered good enough for every day. Nearly everyone, of course, was in the same fix. To point out mended rips and patched elbows and to joke about them was fashionable. It was also fashionable to raise eyebrows at the wardrobes of some members of the Wentworth, Wendell, Langdon, and Pepperell families, and a point of honor never to cast longing looks toward those well-dressed women riding in their coaches.

"Not the next-door Whipples," Priscilla said again. "Or Captain William either, with his slaves and all. These Whipples, I think, used to live over Odiorne's Point way. In fact, I think I remember his father worked on Flake Hill and lived there too."

"Whose father?" Betsy asked absently, her mind now taken up with a frayed cuff. "Look at this, Pris. It can't be shortened or turned one more time. I tell you, I'm in rags."

"Josiah Whipple's father."

"Oh, him." Betsy folded the bodice angrily and stuffed it hastily in a dresser drawer. "I will not wear that tattered thing out in public one more time, and I shall tell Mother so."

"Yes, him. Do you remember him, Betsy?"

"A great oaf, with hair like a haystack? I remember we used to wonder if there really wasn't straw mixed up in it somehow, he seemed such a farmer. Yes, I remember him, in a way. Daniel seemed to know him for some reason. Whatever made you think of him, Pris? Because of the new coach, I suppose. You must have seen him ride in it?"

"What new coach?" Priscilla went on plaiting her hair into a long smooth pigtail, her eyes never leaving her sister's face. "You mean that Josiah Whipple has a coach? I thought he was poor as poor, before. He did all sorts of odd jobs, if I remember rightly. Even worked at Stavers' stable for a while, taking care of the horses and cleaning out the stage chair when it came to town Friday evening. If his father worked at drying fish, and he took care of horses, they are not likely to own a coach now, are they?

You must be thinking of someone else, Betsy."

"No, I'm not," Betsy said indifferently. "I happened over to see Sarah, and we went walking together. She has been poorly, you know, and her father thought a turn in the fresh air would do her good after being shut up within doors for so long. Sarah told me it all began with a pain in her chest. Every time she took a deep breath it bothered her. Do you know, for the last day or two I have had exactly the same thing."

"Oh, Betsy!" cried Priscilla in exasperation. It had been many months since Betsy had complained of an ill or ache first experienced by Sarah Wendell. "Tell me about the coach."

"There's nothing to tell. It was a new coach—new to me, I mean—and Sarah had not seen it before, having been confined to the house for several weeks, but she felt sure it was the one her father had described to her as belonging to the Whipples. Yes, now that I think about it, she did say they had formerly lived at Odiorne's Point, and perhaps did still. But they had all at once bought a house either there or in Kittery, I'm not quite sure which, and had this coach which had been made for John Newmarch, who would not need it because he has gone to fight on one side or another in this stupid war. Oh la, I am so tired and yet when I get to bed, I will not sleep a wink, I know."

Priscilla climbed into bed beside her sister, her mind working furiously. It would do no good to ask Betsy more questions. As she did every night, in spite of her vigorous protestations, Betsy would go immediately to sleep. Besides, Betsy probably knew nothing more of Josiah Whipple anyway. Priscilla felt that more should be known. For a man once concerned with as unprofitable—she supposed —a business as the drying of fish to buy a new or almost-new painted and varnished coach seemed an impossibility. And a house as well? He must be getting money from some fresh and undoubtedly shady source. She had seen Josiah at Sheafe's warehouse, after dark, lurking about stealthily when no one was there. To be sure, he had *said* he was waiting for Mr. Sheafe . . .

"Oh!" Priscilla gasped aloud, and Betsy stirred and murmured complainingly in her sleep. That, of course, was the answer. Just exactly what she had been looking for, and she had almost failed to recognize it under her very nose. Mr. Sheafe was a Tory. He had a warehouse on the waterfront filled with such a clutter of things no one in the world would know if anything unusual was there. He could very well be storing, temporarily, kegs of gunpowder mixed in with those of meal and molasses. There could be stacks of guns concealed under piles of canvas, or—or anything else. He would want someone to transport these contraband supplies, and Josiah Whipple was there to do it. Probably he had a boat tied up below the warehouse . . . Perhaps she had surprised him in the very act of loading it!

Priscilla was so pleased to have found her traitor that she forgot to work out a plan for catching him and went to sleep happily. Now, she said to herself in her last waking moment, she would have something to write to Mark about . . .

Even if she had made plans, Priscilla could not have put them into effect. Almost immediately after her discovery of Josiah Whipple in the warehouse, three of her small sisters fell seriously ill. Priscilla, as well as Betsy and their mother, spent weary hours trying to soothe and comfort them, watching over them each night, waiting anxiously for the doctor's visits. When the last to recover, Mary, had finally taken a turn for the better, Mrs. Purcell, worn out with nursing and with worry, became ill herself. It wasn't until the end of May that she declared herself well again and able to take charge of her household.

Priscilla felt worn out as well, after all the desperate weeks, but she forced herself into writing frequent notes to Mark. The small letters would, she hoped, pile up on a dock or ship and reach him all at once, making up in their number what each lacked in news and interest. Writing to Mark always seemed to bring her nearer to the Captain. As she wrote she found that she was more aware of Mark too, more anxious to make him feel that someone at home had him in mind and cared what was happening to him. No matter how hard he tried to disguise it, his infrequent letters always made her realize that he suffered much from homesickness, even though he had no home.

When news came to Portsmouth, it was first good and then bad. The *Ranger* had fought the *Drake*, after cruising to the Irish Sea and engaging in skirmishes with ships whose names meant nothing and off shores that the people in Portsmouth knew little of. It was exciting to know that the *Ranger* had won a hard-fought battle with a twenty-gun sloop of war, but the good news was tempered with bad. Five of the *Ranger's* men were wounded and three, including Lieutenant Samuel Wallingford, about whom both Daniel and Mark had written with much admiration, had been killed. Betsy, as worn out with nursing as Priscilla, took to her bed at the very thought of how close Daniel might have come to being one of the casualties. Nothing either Priscilla or their mother could do would arouse her.

"Perhaps it's just as well to let her stay there a while,"

Mrs. Purcell said at last. "The rest will do her good. I can't bear to hear my child sob so, but sooner or later she'll get over that."

"I hope so." Priscilla was impatient with her sister, but for once she sympathized with her, finding herself concerned over Mark's safety to a surprising degree. When at last more news trickled back to Portsmouth, they learned of the Captain's successes off the Irish coast. There were many tales of heroism to give the town satisfaction, and to Priscilla's surprise, Mark Jaffrey was mentioned several times as having helped the Captain in his daring deeds. Daniel even wrote to Betsy that Captain Paul Jones had asked for a reward for Mark, among others, and Priscilla felt a very personal glow of pride.

"It's maddening to receive the letters so long after things happen!" Betsy exclaimed. She had been restored to health when Daniel's long letters appeared. "But Daniel says they may come home soon. At any rate, their term of enlistment is up on the first of October, and that's only a little over four months away."

"Only!" said Priscilla grumpily. "What do you mean, only?"

"It's better than a year or something," Betsy reminded her. "What's happened to us, Pris? I'm usually the pessimist."

Priscilla nodded. While Betsy had four letters from Daniel to pore over, Priscilla had only one brief note from Mark, and she found herself worrying more than she had thought possible. Was she worrying over Mark's safety or over whether or not he had, for one reason or another, lost interest in her? She was ashamed of herself.

"No wonder," she told herself, slamming copper pots about carelessly as she worked at the spring housecleaning that was so late in getting done this year. "No wonder. All I ever wrote to him was how everybody in the house was sick. What kind of cheerful mail is that? And what happened to my plan to be a heroine, to have something really interesting to put in a letter?"

That very day she waited until the rest of the household was busy with serving supper to the boarders and slipped away. Hannah had reluctantly taken her place once again with Betsy and Priscilla, leaving Mary to watch over Susan and Maggie. The extra pair of hands lightened the load considerably. Priscilla knew she wouldn't be missed. The warm May weather had restored sagging spirits, and as she left the house Caddie and Molly were cackling away at some joke, Jerusha was singing off-key as she prepared for the washing up, and Betsy and Hannah were engaged in one of the verbal sparring contests they seemed to enjoy so much.

Priscilla hurried along Pitt Street toward the waterfront. The afternoon hours were still cool, although the days were warm. She had worn her winter cloak and now found it much too heavy. Still, she didn't want to slow her steps, so she tossed it behind her as she sped along, holding it together at her throat and wishing she dared take it off altogether. It was not yet dark. She wondered if anyone saw her almost running down the street and tried to think what she would say if someone asked her where she was going at such a pace. Suppose Mr. Sheafe or anyone else was at the warehouse and wanted to know why she was there. She hadn't seen Dorothey for nearly two weeks, but decided to use her again as an excuse if it was necessary.

"I was to meet my friend here, sir," she would say to Mr. Sheafe. "Have you seen her? Dorothy Hall, I mean." The fact that Dorothy was always needed at the Colonel's tavern at this hour made it a fairly poor excuse, but Priscilla could think of no other. After all, not everyone in town knows about Dorothy's daily schedule, she told herself hopefully.

It was almost dark when she hurried the last few yards and pushed open the door of the warehouse. For the first time she wondered what she would have done had the door been locked. Wouldn't it be locked, if Mr. Sheafe had gone home for the evening? Come to think of it, it had been open the other time too. Surely he must lock the place at night, with all of that merchandise in there, and the fittings and gear for boats and ships, all in such short supply these days?

Priscilla stifled a sigh and crept carefully across the wooden floor, watching in the dim light for obstacles that might make her trip and reveal her presence. At the very back of the building there was a wide-open door. Through it she could see the river, dull silver in the fading light. Over the lapping of the water, she heard another sound, the kind of noise made by heavy rope sliding on wood. There was a light too, a very faint light that seemed to shine from below. With her heart in her mouth, she crept along the vast shadow of the building, feeling her way as she went, exploring with her toe for the next place to put her foot.

Suddenly there was a bump, as if a small boat banged against the heavy wet piles supporting the building, and a muttered exclamation of pain. The big door over the water was illuminated as a hand reached up and deposited a lantern on the floor. The lantern was followed by a head and then, as he heaved himself up from below, the big body of Josiah Whipple.

Priscilla's heart was beating so hard she thought it could

be heard for miles. As Josiah scrambled to his feet, he raised the lantern and, unaccountably, looked right at her.

"You again, Miss Elizabeth Purcell?" he exclaimed.

"I—I'm Priscilla." Her voice shook with fright and excitement. "What—what are you doing here, Josiah?"

"Why, I'm the watchman," he said cheerfully. "Not much of a one, I guess, if you can break in here and me not know it."

"You know it," she said shortly.

"Only because you stand there in plain sight," he said with a grin. "Guess I better poke around in the corners. What do you think? Suppose anybody else is in here?"

Priscilla shivered and looked around fearfully at the shapes and shadows.

"I can see you hope there ain't. So do I. Want something?" he asked abruptly.

"No, I—I was looking for—someone." It suddenly occurred to her that she owed him no explanation. "I—I guess I'll go home now."

She hurried away, wishing that the light of his lantern was not directly behind her. She created a huge shadow that made it impossible to see the cluttered floor clearly, but she wanted to get away as quickly as possible. Something was very, very wrong in Josiah's presence there, she was sure. But even though she had found him in the warehouse twice and believed him to be stealing or smuggling or both, how could she prove it? To whom should she tell her fears? Not Mr. Sheafe, certainly, since Josiah was probably there under his orders. Her mother? That would expose her own part in it, and her mother would certainly frown on that! If only the Captain were here, or Mark, or even Daniel. Mr. Wendell, Daniel's father? Perhaps she could tell him, or have Betsy tell him, but that would involve letting Betsy in on her part and Betsy would be sure to tattle to their mother.

Priscilla flew along the dark street, running homeward even faster than she had toward the waterfront. Her mind churned as she hurried. By the time she had reached the Purcell garden, where she paused to catch her breath, she had decided to fall back on Dorothy, even though Dorothy was so preoccupied with the young man from Salem. Dorothy could ask Colonel Stoodley what to do. That was the only solution.

With that settled and her breathing almost back to normal, Priscilla straightened her cloak, smoothed her hair back under her bonnet, and walked demurely to the house. There was no one about as she quietly closed the front door, and she was able to get rid of her wraps without anyone seeing her. She thought to hurry upstairs to her room, which would give her time to think, but as she put her hand on the carved newel-post she felt it give under her fingers and paused to tighten it. At one time, when her father was alive, the deed to the house and other papers had been inserted in the hollow post, but her mother had removed them, Priscilla knew. As a hiding place it was less than satisfactory, since so many people did the same thing.

Intent on replacing the top of the hollow post properly, she was only vaguely aware that chairs were being scraped backward in the dining room to her right. Half consciously she thought, I have been to the warehouse, met a spy, and come home again, and all they have done in there is eat Caddie's supper. . . .

The door opened and Mr. Mason walked through, giving her one of his quick, shy little bows. Priscilla ducked her head politely and was about to turn away when she heard one of the men say, "So, Jacob, you are your own night watchman these days?"

Priscilla looked over Mr. Mason's head. Jacob? It was — it was Mr. Sheafe! She stood rooted to the spot, waiting for his answer.

"Let us say merely that if there is a night watchman, I am he," Mr. Sheafe said. "Benny shipped out on the *Swallow*, without so much as a word to me. Took the place of someone who had jumped ship, they tell me, so the offer was quick made and quick taken, no doubt. He will soon find that serving as a member of a crew on a broad-beamed sloop that wallows in a heavy sea is more difficult than sleeping in the corner on a pile of sacks, although he professed not to be able to close his eyes at night, so full of noises is my warehouse. Well, as I told you, there have been no alarms along the waterfront lately. I make surprise visits to my property every so often, and that will have to do until I can find someone to take Benny's place. Or until he comes back and begs for his old berth again."

Priscilla picked up her skirts and fled up the stairs, leaving the men standing below and finishing their supper conversation. It was uncanny that Mr. Sheafe should be supping at her house this very night, even more so that he should discuss, in her hearing, the watchman question that so plagued her. Now she *knew* that Josiah Whipple had no right to be at the warehouse. At least that much was clear, although knowing what to do about it was not.

She forgot even that burning question, temporarily, when she heard the latest report. Captain John Paul Jones had "given up" the *Ranger*. He was waiting, it was said, for another ship, perhaps *L'Indien* of which they had heard earlier, but at any rate a finer one than the *Ranger*. Veiled hints and some outright statements convinced the people at home that there had been trouble between the Captain and Lieutenant Simpson—more trouble, serious trouble. But not even the greatest gossips seemed disposed to write much about it in letters. At any rate, so many of the men professed relief at the change that Priscilla wondered what could have happened. Whatever it was, she was sure the Captain was in the right. He was known as a stern disciplinarian, and everyone agreed that people never took kindly to discipline. It all had to do with that, no doubt.

She was deeply concerned, though, about the news that the Captain himself would not be returning, although it was planned to send the *Ranger* home soon. Many who had sailed with the Captain would be aboard, Dorothy's uncle and, Betsy prayed, her eyes squeezed tight with longing, Daniel Wendell, since Daniel was supposed to remain with Lieutenant Simpson.

No one besides herself, Priscilla thought, cared whether or not Midshipman Mark Jaffrey would be on the *Ranger* when she sailed into port. Because of Mark's great admiration for Captain Jones she feared he might go with him. No one knew when the *Ranger* would leave France. "Soon" was the word most commonly used, although one or two claimed they had heard "this summer." "It's almost June. Perhaps the *Ranger* is preparing even now to sail," Betsy exclaimed, in a rare moment of optimism. "Daniel could be home in four or five weeks. Imagine!"

Since the Captain wasn't coming back, and presumably Mark wasn't either, Priscilla decided, when the excitement had died down, that now was the time to carry out her plans. Her first step was to tell Dorothy about it. She found Dorothy singularly uninterested.

"I never did like that Josiah Whipple," she said. "He's so

big, and so untidy-looking. The way he stares at you with those light eyes—it gives a body the shivers. But even if he is doing wrong, I don't see how you can hope to catch him, all by yourself."

"I can't. That's why I'm telling you all this," Priscilla said impatiently. "I want your help."

"What could *I* do?"

"You can tell Colonel Stoodley about it, and he could advise us. Or have some men go and catch Josiah there, if he thinks that's best."

"Well, I won't tell him," Dorothy said flatly. "He'd laugh at us, Pris. He thinks we're 'silly gels' anyway, he's always saying so."

"Then we must go ourselves," Priscilla announced.

"You won't catch me creeping around that old warehouse at night," Dorothy said flatly. "I don't even like to go in there in the daytime. Besides, it smells of fish and tar and a whole lot of awful things."

"If you're going to catch a spy, you have to put up with a few little things like funny smells," Priscilla said loftily.

"Spy? Last time you said he was a traitor. Which is he?"

"I don't know. What does it matter?" Priscilla had used the words interchangeably in her mind and she had never thought about it before. "He must be smuggling things to the British, probably he's both."

Dorothy shrugged indifferently. Priscilla thought she saw a crafty look cross her friend's face, but it was gone so quickly she might have imagined it.

"You wouldn't mind if Samuel came with us, would you? We'd need a man, I'm sure."

"Samuel who? Oh, Samuel Otis." Priscilla had at last met the young man from Salem. He was slight and slender, with white hands and a shy, hesitant voice. Compared to Mark or Daniel, he was pretty poor material, Priscilla thought. She couldn't imagine him on board the *Ranger*, for example, doing a man's work.

However, it was likely that she would get Dorothy with Samuel or not at all, so she said as shortly as she could, "I think that would be a good idea, Dorothy. Do you—would he come?"

"He will if I ask him to," Dorothy retorted with a toss of her head. "When, Pris?"

"Tomorrow evening, I think." Priscilla mentally reviewed the plans for the next day. There was a meeting of some kind in the afternoon at the William Pitt, and most if not all of her mother's boarders would not be at home at suppertime. "You tell your Aunt Elizabeth you are coming to my house for supper, and I will tell my mother I am going to yours," she said.

"But where will we have supper?" Dorothy objected.

"Oh, dear, you do hate missing a meal," Priscilla teased her. "It wouldn't hurt you much either. That bodice seems tight to me. Well, can't you and your Samuel worry something out of the kitchen before you leave? We can meet at the Liberty Pole at—at six o'clock?"

"It won't be dark."

"No, but we must be careful not to be out after curfew. Tomorrow then?"

"Tomorrow." Dorothy's face showed pleasure, but Priscilla sensed it was because she would be spending extra time with her Samuel, not because she would be doing something heroic for her country. "Tomorrow night, at six, Pris. We'll be there."

Chapter 11

TO CATCH A SPY

PRISCILLA WOKE UP the next morning wondering how she had ever got herself into the clandestine trip to the warehouse, and her dread of the adventure grew throughout the day. If she hadn't been so busy at home helping her mother straighten out some tangled accounts, she would have run over to the tavern and told Dorothy that she'd changed her mind.

Perhaps Dorothy will change her mind, she thought hopefully, until she remembered the pleasure Dorothy was taking in it simply because her precious Samuel was involved. As the afternoon drew to a close, she began to wonder how she was to escape from the house, but her mother said, "We are free as birds tonight, Priscilla. The guests won't be here, not a one of them. I gave Caddie the evening off, and Molly and Jerusha too. I am going to run down to see Molly Shortridge and will sup with her, if she'll have me. She thinks to open a boardinghouse one day too, and has many questions for me. I ask you girls to fend for yourselves tonight, if you don't mind.

"I think you will all enjoy a little variety in your lives," Mrs. Purcell went on. "Hannah has agreed to feed the younger ones, and perhaps will prepare something for you too, if you wish."

"No, no, thank you. I—" There was no need to tell her fib, Priscilla realized, and she stopped short of saying she would eat at Dorothy's. Mrs. Purcell didn't seem to notice that the sentence hadn't been finished, and Priscilla fled to her room to get ready. It was only five o'clock, but she sensed she should get out of the house before some complication presented itself.

Betsy was there, moping as usual, because no word had come from Daniel for so long.

"Why don't you go see Sarah?" Priscilla suggested. "Perhaps she'll ask you to tea, as I believe the Wendells are pleased to call supper. We are free as birds, Mother just said so. I for one am going to take advantage of this opportunity. How often are we 'free as birds,' I want to know!"

Betsy brightened up immediately. Trust Betsy, Priscilla thought, not to ask questions. She never sees beyond the end of her nose. I could be sailing for England, and she wouldn't notice, unless she fell over my trunk in the hallway.

Betsy changed her clothes so hurriedly that she was ready to leave before Priscilla, and Priscilla, although glad of the few moments of solitude, was not inclined to linger, lest Hannah ask for help with the children or the supper. No matter how hard she tried, she couldn't imagine the scene ahead. Would Josiah run from them? Would he stand his ground and jeer at them? Would he penitently hang his head and agree that he had been doing wrong? If so, he could certainly be marched straight to the jail, and the matter would be ended. Except, of course, for the glory. She could see herself writing to Mark: "You are not the only person who is fighting in this stupid war. You won't believe this, I suppose, but I—with the help of Dorothy Hall and a friend of hers—actually captured a spy." Wouldn't the Captain smile at that, when Mark told him? And be proud of her too?

Even while she spun the pretty dream in her head, she really knew how ridiculous it was to suppose that Mark and Captain Jones should take time out to read a letter from home together. Perhaps they never exchanged a word on deck, except for giving and taking orders. Still, every sentence she wrote was subtly shaped for the Captain's ears or eyes, even though she admitted to herself that she was being a silly girl.

The position of the shadow on the floor told her that time was running by quickly. She pulled on her light-weight cloak, wound a kerchief about her head in lieu of a bonnet, and was ready. When she reached the bottom of the stairway, she found the children eating at the kitchen table and chattering gleefully. They were accustomed to having supper in their room, and bread and milk seemed far more tasty in blue-and-white bowls in the big kitchen. Even the baby was gurgling with pleasure and taking from Hannah each spoonful without demur. It struck Priscilla that she scarcely knew her smaller sisters. She should have some of the fun—and headache too, she supposed—of bringing them up, but the Purcells were always so busy, with no time left over to be a proper and loving family.

Hannah looked up at her older sister with a smile. "A change is good for us all, I think," she said. "Mary has been fussing about how hard it is to get them to eat lately, and look at them now. Where are you off to?"

"Dorothy's," Priscilla flung back over her shoulder. "Good night, babies."

The streets were golden with light from the west as she

hurried along. Now she was forgetting her dreams. The experience ahead represented a vast, unknown quantity, and there could well be danger involved. She shivered and drew her cloak around her more closely. It was a stupid idea, really. Well, she must own up to it as soon as she saw Dorothy, and they had better all go home and try to forget about it. Perhaps the others won't even come, she thought hopefully. Then Dorothy won't have to know that I turned into a coward at the last minute.

Just as she reached the Liberty Pole, she saw two figures approaching from the opposite direction, and her heart sank down into her boots. There was no escape after all, at least not without an admission of cowardice. She put on as brave a smile as she could manage and hurried to meet them. Samuel Otis was bending toward Dorothy in a very gallant way, looking down into her face ardently, and Dorothy wore the look of a cat who has just found and lapped up a whole saucer of cream. Priscilla felt a spurt of anger and even envy. She didn't really like this Samuel with his long eyelashes and his girlish ways, but it was better having Samuel look at you that way than having no one.

Dorothy gave her a languid wave, as though they were meeting by chance instead of appointment.

"Good evening, Priscilla," she called, when they drew near. "It is most pleasant tonight, is it not?"

Priscilla glared at her friend. "Most pleasant"—really! Why should Dorothy put on such airs of a sudden, pretending to be a young lady of fashion casually meeting an acquaintance on the street.

Samuel Otis smiled pleasantly enough and bowed his head, but he too appeared to think they all just happened to be there.

"Well," said Priscilla brusquely, forgetting that she had meant to call the expedition off, "shall we get on with it?" Come to think of it, she decided, I don't sound like myself either!

"On with it?" Samuel looked surprised. He glanced at Dorothy questioningly.

"I didn't tell you," Dorothy said brightly, with a false giggle, "but we are here on a mission. One that Priscilla has cooked up for us, Samuel. We wanted you along because we frail young women feel the need of a strong man, don't we, Pris?"

"Mission?" The question on his face had turned to bewilderment. "Mission? Here?"

Priscilla turned and gestured toward the warehouse. "There," she said shortly. "At Mr. Sheafe's. We're going to —to catch a—well, a spy or something. Didn't you tell him, Dorothy?"

"No," said Dorothy quickly. "I thought Samuel would enjoy a little mystery. I just suggested we take a walk. The evening is so fine, and—"

Samuel Otis was regarding Priscilla fixedly. His blue eyes narrowed. They had become steely and cold.

"I think perhaps," he said, "you had better tell me what you are up to. I don't care to take part in any spy chase, or whatever it is, without at least knowing what it's all about."

"Priscilla is the one to tell you," Dorothy said hastily. "It's all her idea."

Priscilla looked at the cold eyes and said sharply, "It's a body's duty, nowadays, to keep an eye out for spies and smugglers, or for anyone that might hurt our cause. I'm sure you agree."

"But I want to know what it is you have discovered,

Miss Priscilla. Something must have set you on this quest, but you haven't yet told me what it is."

Priscilla bit her lip. It sounded like such a small thing, spelled out, and she was conscious of a blush mounting to her cheeks.

"There is someone who comes to Mr. Sheafe's warehouse," she said, and her tongue felt stiff and unwieldy. "Mr. Sheafe is, of course, a Tory, we all know that because he makes no bones about it. But he has never been active, so far as anyone has found out. However, someone is probably smuggling things out of the warehouse at night, either with or without Mr. Sheafe's knowledge."

"What do you propose to do about it?"

"Why—why, c-c-catch him at it," Priscilla stammered. "Confront him, I suppose. And turn him over to—to the authorities."

Samuel threw back his head and laughed.

"What do you find so comical in that?" she demanded, stung. "That someone is stealing from us, pray?"

"No. No. I beg your pardon, Miss Priscilla. You looked so—so determined, that is all. I find it commendable, but—well, if I may speak frankly, I believe perhaps this—this great and heroic and patriotic deed needs more thought and preparation. And of course I would be delighted to be of service. Suppose that we meet—say, tomorrow afternoon, at Dorothy's. By that time I will have done a little judicious checking about the town and be better prepared for the—the—kill, shall we say? Do you agree, Miss Priscilla? And you, Miss Dorothy, my dear?"

Dorothy, Priscilla thought with a stifled snort, would have agreed to anything, with those blue eyes gazing at her so soulfully. As for herself, she was so filled with the surge of relief that she could only nod and say briefly, "I'll be over tomorrow, Dorothy." She gathered her cloak about her and swirled away, unwilling to watch their eyes meeting and holding with such ardor. She knew what it was to be gazed at like that—hadn't the Captain looked at her that way once?

Curiously, it was not the Captain who seemed to hurry beside her as she hastened home, but Mark. The brown eyes she imagined were Mark's. Mark's eyes were not as dark as the Captain's, and much softer when they looked at her. And Mark had bent toward her in the same way and paid her much the same courteous attention that Samuel bestowed on Dorothy. How odd, she thought, that I never realized it before. Hurrying along, she decided to start a letter to Mark as soon as she got home. The—the adventure could be added, later. Right now she wanted to pass along to Mark some warmth and affection. She had been far too impersonal and chilly in her letters. Her feeling for the Captain had not altered in any way, it was just that she had suddenly found room for two men in her life.

The next day was rainy, and cold for June. The children were fretful and cranky, and the whole family had its hands full.

"Why didn't you put them to bed when you should have?" Priscilla exclaimed. "You said you wanted to give them a treat. I think it was your own treat, because you had them to yourself for once."

"Maybe it was," Hannah flared out at her. "It's all very well for you and Betsy to make me help you with your work. You don't mind it, but I like to be with the children."

"Who says we don't mind it!" scolded Betsy. "We hate it, Hannah Purcell, just as much as you do."

"Who does enjoy herself in this house," Priscilla grumbled, "for that matter."

"Susan." Mary, unfailingly good-natured, had just come

into the parlor. "But soon we'll pull her out of her crib and make her dust the feet of all of the furniture, and the legs as far as she can reach, and she will complain just like the rest of us!"

"You don't complain, Mary," Priscilla said generously. "This household is certainly out of sorts today, what with the children and the rain. I must go to Dorothy's this afternoon, so if someone will work it out with me, I'll do double duty this morning. This is important, it is not just a whim," she added hastily.

To her surprise they accepted her statement equably, and fell to discussing a rearrangement of duties. As a result, toward the end of the afternoon Priscilla found herself free. Wrapping herself against the rain, she escaped from the house before her mother began to ask questions or found a way to prevent her leaving.

The dusty streets had turned to mud, and the cart tracks were deep, slowing her considerably. She was well soaked when she finally burst through the door of Stoodley's Tavern. Taking off her wet outer garments carefully, she looked about her as usual at the wide central hall, with its spacious stairway rising on the right wall. She had been in all rooms on the first floor at one time or another, and invariably admired the wainscoting in each. Priscilla had never been inside either the Bell or the William Pitt, but she understood that for sheer fineness of appointments and design, neither could touch Colonel Stoodley's. The rooms upstairs, which she had glimpsed, were rich-looking too. Each had its own fireplace like the rooms downstairs. Above them was the assembly room, used for dances and parties, which impressed her too, although Dorothy always assured her that the large hall was much plainer than the other rooms.

"But you should see it," Dorothy had told her, "when the

ladies in their silks and the men in their best coats and ruf-
fles are dancing there! The room *must* be simple, you see,
to serve as background for such finery. Colonel James explained that to me once."

It was odd, Priscilla thought, as she admired the hallway, that Dorothy was not here to meet her. It was the
first time her friend hadn't been at the door, to drag her
away to kitchen or parlor, or to her own room tucked at
the back of the second floor. Of course Dorothy hadn't
known the exact time of her arrival. Still, Dorothy had a
way of running to the window just frequently enough
when Priscilla was expected to catch a glimpse of her and
be ready at the door.

Priscilla stood in the hallway uncertainly. She did not
hear even the usual sounds of the place—the loud laughter
of men grouped about a table lingering over their large
dinners, the cries as lobsters fresh roasted on grills in the
fireplaces were served, the sound of pots and pans and
crockery in the big kitchen, and the murmuring of Dorothy's aunt and the women who helped her there. No door
slammed, no fire crackled and popped. There was only the
sighing of the wind outside and the steady beat of the rain
on the small panes of the windows.

Priscilla tried to shake off a sudden chill that swept over
her. It was like walking into a haunted house, a house that
harbored ghosts instead of people. She found it frightening. Afraid and yet determined, she walked almost stealthily toward the door that led to the kitchen. If there was
anyone at all in the tavern, he would be there, she was sure
of it. As she pushed the door open, cautiously and with a
fast-beating heart, she heard a sound at last—a sound not
in the least ghostlike, but entirely human. It was the sound
of a person sobbing her heart out. Stepping around the

door Priscilla saw that it was Dorothy, who was half sitting and half lying in a carved wooden chair. Bending over her was her Aunt Elizabeth.

"It's you. I never want to see you again. Get away from here, go away, go away!"

Priscilla stopped in her tracks, openmouthed. Dorothy's face was wet with tears and so swollen that Priscilla knew the weeping had been going on for some time.

"B-but Dorothy, what has happened?"

"Go away, go away, go away!" Dorothy sobbed, cradling her head on her arms.

Priscilla looked at Mrs. Hall, who shook her head sadly and turned back to Dorothy.

"It is not Priscilla's fault," she said sharply. "Indeed, you should be thanking your friend, miss, not blaming her. Supposing she had not uncovered this dreadful thing, answer me that! Yes indeed, instead of sitting there and wailing and shouting at your best friend to leave your house, you ought to be down on your knees telling her how grateful you are. Do you hear me, Dorothy?"

Dorothy continued to wail, but at least she had stopped talking.

"I don't understand," Priscilla cried. "What has happened. Where is Samuel—Mr. Otis?"

There was a fresh torrent of tears at that, and Priscilla began to understand that the gentleman from Salem was certainly at the bottom of the trouble, whatever it was. She could think of nothing to say, but decided to wait until someone told her what it was all about.

"Mr. Otis—if that is his name—and Mr. Neale, as he calls himself, have gone. From what I can get out of this creature here, who hasn't spoke a sensible pair of words since it happened, we have you to thank for it. I for one do thank you, and so does Colonel James, although he isn't here to speak for himself."

Priscilla found her knees unwilling to hold her up any longer. Uninvited, she sank down on a chair.

"Mr. Samuel Otis, and Mr. John Neale, uncle and nephew they told me, from Salem and here to look over the rope walks. It sounded right enough, since Portsmouth always has been a center for shipbuilding and that means ropes must be made. You know how the men carry the ropes through the streets looking like centipedes as they go."

Priscilla had heard Dorothy complain of her aunt's talking too much, and sometimes even mimic the torrent of words. But this was the first time she had been so suffocated by the sheer volume of sound. Dorothy's snuffling and sniffing was relatively quiet.

"Anyway, it all sounded well enough, and no one thought to ask questions, not even my father, and he is often suspicious of people for no cause at all. They stayed here. They were quiet gentlemen and they came and went peaceably enough. They paid for their room and their meals, and no one thought twice about them. Until now, and we all put our heads together and realized that they were great ones for questions. The young one, with his pretty face and hands, he pays much attention to poor Dorothy, but he asks her about this person or that, and who owns this house, and where such and such a ship might be tied up, and what kind of cargo it might carry. And Dorothy, poor silly girl, she tells him everything she knows."

Dorothy burst into angry sobs that subsided almost at once, as though she was about sobbed out.

"Which fortunately wasn't much," Mrs. Hall went on

dryly. "But nonetheless, he must have learned something from her. And Colonel James—well, my father is not one who likes to be taken in, and when he realized that he too had passed along information to the older one—that Mr. Neale—he all but reached for his musket. I had to talk to him sharp, so I did. He went out and the others with him, but without guns. It doesn't matter now anyway, because there is no doubt but that the fine pair are halfway to Salem. Or rather, more likely to Halifax, where they will join their kind."

"But—" Priscilla could make no sense out of the words, even though there were so many of them.

"Don't you see, they cared about rope walks no more than you or I. As Colonel James says now, although he did not think of it before—that he admits to me—a man can stare at rope walks in Salem, or in Newburyport, or Salisbury Point, or many other places. But no, they must come to Portsmouth, and us so flattered we believed what they told us! Now we see they were sent here to search out their Tory friends and arouse them, to get them to stop living with us peaceably as they chose to do and have done, so far as we know, all this time. And especially they were here to send out any arms or whatever might be lying around, to pass them on to their loyalist friends up north. And you stopped them."

"But I don't see how I—"

"You and Dorothy took that young man down to the very scene of his activity, so to speak, and from what Dorothy said you as much as told him that you knew what he was up to."

"But I didn't! I thought—"

"You didn't, and you know it. And we know it. But Mr. Samuel Otis and Mr. John Neale, neither of them knew it.

They thought you were onto them, you see. And they ske-daddled, the pair of them, in the dead of the night. Went down to Stavers' and took their horses and were gone, quick as you please. The funny thing is, they left money here for me, what they owed, and at Stavers' stable too. Villains, the pair of them, but they must pay their debts!"

"He's not a villain," cried Dorothy damply, speaking for the first time in quite a while. "He was—sweet, and nice and he—he loved me. He told me so."

"I doubt if he spoke the truth." Mrs. Hall's voice was un-expectedly gentle. "I'm afraid it was part of his little game, Dorothy. Well, one day you will understand, and you'll find that you don't mind. You may even enjoy remember-ing that you were made sport of by a traitor to your coun-try. You are not the only girl in the colonies who has been the target of such a man, I promise you. Oh, I'm sorry, child, it hurts now, of course it does. But it won't hurt long. You wait and see, you—you and Priscilla—will be a pair of heroines in this town."

"Everybody will—l-laugh at me!" Dorothy wailed. "I can't bear it."

"They won't laugh. They don't know you were taken in by a pair of blue eyes and eyelashes long enough to make any girl in the world green with envy. No one knows, ex-cept Priscilla and me. And Colonel James, of course, but he is fond of you too and none of us will tell. Will we, Pris-cilla?"

"He is?" Dorothy mopped her eyes and looked at her aunt hopefully.

"Fond of you? My father? Why yes, indeed he is. He's gruff, and he barks at people. But he is as fond of you as though you were his own flesh and blood. We all are, Dor-othy. Perhaps we should take time to tell you."

Dorothy's blue eyes were pink-rimmed, and the flesh around them was puffed, but Priscilla could see how pleased she was at her aunt's words. Priscilla smiled warmly at Mrs. Hall for having cheered Dorothy up when she needed it so badly. Dorothy's aunt nodded curtly and left the room, a plump little figure bustling and trotting as usual, and Priscilla saw with surprise as she passed that Mrs. Hall's eyes were wet too.

"Well," Priscilla said, "I'm really awfully sorry, Dorothy. I didn't mean for things to turn out this way."

Dorothy blew her nose loudly and smoothed back her dark, straight hair.

"I—it really isn't so bad, Pris. I mean, he—he—I wasn't absolutely—well, to be perfectly truthful with you, I sometimes didn't even *like* him. He was so—so sort of soft, you know. But he paid me so much attention, you see, and no one ever had before. To be truthful, he didn't really say he *loved* me, Pris, but— Well, Aunt Elizabeth is right, I will get over it. And it wasn't your fault. Imagine them, living right here in our house!" she marveled. She stood up, smoothed down her skirts, and twitched her bodice into place. "Imagine! Pris, did you hear what she said? That they are fond of me, they like me. Even Colonel James. I thought they just—well, you know, put up with me because they had to."

Priscilla looked at the face still shining with recent tears and thought that she shouldn't be so surprised at the sudden change in climate. Dorothy had always been matter-of-fact and cheerful. Catching those scoundrels isn't the only good thing that has come out of all this, she told herself, satisfied now that Dorothy would not suffer from a broken—or even a cracked—heart. Oh, I will have so much to write about, in my next letter to Mark!

Chapter 12

ECHOES OF BATTLE

THE BUSINESS of scaring away Colonel Stoodley's "guests from Salem," as they were always called, was the talk of the town for a few days. Priscilla often thought she and Dorothy should have been praised a bit more frequently and loudly, but somehow their part in the escapade soon became lost as the story made its rounds, picking up color and embroidery as it went. By mid-July to her disgust the whole world had forgotten. The only consolation was that it did, for a few hours, keep her busy writing a fat and, she hoped, interesting letter to Mark.

In October the *Ranger* sailed back into the harbor. Most of the town was on the shore to greet her, as soon as word got around that she was coming. Priscilla, Dorothy, Betsy, Augusta, and Helen looked for their flag.

"Even if it looks like ours," Helen said nervously, "he might have had a copy made."

"It is the old one, the Grand Union Jack," said Mary Langdon, who joined the group at that moment. She looked, Priscilla thought resentfully, like a lady of fashion, with a narrow-brimmed hat in contrast to the wide drooping brims of the hats worn by the others. She won-

dered crossly where soft blue wool, enough to make a coat
and to trim the panels of the silk dress, was to be found
these days. She knew the answer though—Mary's father
had an interest in at least seven ships out privateering on
the sea. Much of his booty would be in the form of silks
and fine wools and plain or printed cottons, dispatched
originally for the loyalists in America who still had money
in their pockets.

The others must have felt as Priscilla did. They all self-
consciously adjusted their bonnets and drew their cloaks
around them.

"He should have sent our flag back with the *Ranger*,"
Augusta said.

"No. We made it for *him*," Helen retorted. It was the
old argument. How long had it been since they'd been
through this before? Six or seven months, Priscilla thought.
But it seems like years. Suddenly moved by the moment—
the shouting, the noises of the busy harbor, the hopeful
and hopeless faces—she felt her eyes fill with tears, and the
silhouette of the *Ranger*, as she was warped into her berth,
was filmed over with quivering rainbows.

Slowly at first, and then in a rush, the men came ashore.
Mary Langdon sailed off on the arm of Peter Wendell, a
distant cousin of Daniel's, and the girls who had been
standing with her blinked. They had not known that Mary
and Peter knew each other more than slightly.

"The war," remarked Helen sadly, "does strange things
to people." Priscilla knew she was thinking not only of a
friendship that must have developed through an exchange
of words inked on paper, but of a marriage in which Helen
had seen her husband for perhaps all of twenty days in a
year and a half or more.

Mark did not come down the gangplank, nor did Daniel.

There would be letters, the watchful women unclaimed by returning men were told. The *Ranger* had brought back letters for everyone in the Province, or so it seemed, and most of them from the men who were no longer on the *Ranger*. The mail would be handed around later. The women, anxious as they were for some word, decided to leave. It was too cold, too gray, too lonely, waiting for a scrawl when one's sister or best friend or neighbor was now strolling along the street on the arm of someone she loved.

Priscilla and Betsy walked home in silence. Their mother, who was waiting at the door, saw at once what had happened.

"I'm sorry, girls," she said gently. "This is a difficult day for you both."

"He had no right not to come!" Betsy cried, breaking her silence with a string of angry words. "He was supposed to stay with Simpson. His father told him to. He has no right to do this."

"Would you have him leave the war when it needs him most?" Sarah Purcell asked her daughter.

Betsy lapsed into sullen silence, and Priscilla stared at her sister, trying to see into her mind. She was proud of Mark for staying on, now that the first pang of learning that he had not come home had left her. She had been surprised at how violent that pang had been and how hard she had looked for him, trying to pick him out in the stream of men who poured out of the ship. But now that it was over, she was swept with pride. Why couldn't Betsy see it the same way?

The next meeting of the Quilting Party was more than five months later. It was Helen Seavey, as usual, who called them together. They were all there but Caroline. She had gone to Philadelphia to be with her fiancé, whose wound was causing him much trouble and had brought on a frightening fever. "They will be married there," Anna announced. "Caroline says she has waited long enough. She says it does not matter how ill William is, either. As his wife she will have a right to stay there and nurse him."

Priscilla looked at Helen, whose face was drawn and gray. She must expect bad news every single day of her life, she thought, and admired the girl for her great effort to be calm and cheerful.

"No doubt you all have had the same intelligence," Helen began, "but since Mr. Fowle had this long talk with Lieutenant Hall—but Dorothy, of course, he is your uncle. You must tell the others."

"Uncle Elijah is not much given to discussing the war at home," Dorothy said with a smile. "Aunt Elizabeth does not like to hear of it, and he has learned to keep silent. I'm sure you know much more than I do about it, Helen. You go ahead."

"Captain Paul Jones—or, I suppose, Commodore, as we should call him now—has another ship. It is French, an East Indiaman, Mr. Fowle told me, and was called *Le Duc de Duras,* if I pronounce it correctly. Not a new ship at all, Mr. Fowle tells me, and not entirely to the Captain's liking. But I suppose, like everyone else, he must make the best of what is offered. He has renamed the ship the *Bonhomme Richard*—after Doctor Franklin, of course." Helen looked around, saw a puzzled frown on Anna's sallow face and added, "Not after him exactly, I suppose, but it is the name Dr. Franklin uses when he writes those almanacs. No, that isn't quite right either, is it. 'Poor Richard' is the name, but his almanacs have been translated into French, and 'Bonhomme Richard' is the French version, Mr. Fowle says. Anyway, when the ship is ready, and heaven knows how long it will take, judging by the way things go around here, it will sail as the *Bonhomme Richard*. And our flag with it!"

"Won't it be grand to hear he has gone off to battle?" Augusta asked Priscilla eagerly when they met by chance one day just in front of the State House. Priscilla shivered, not entirely because of the blast of April wind that swept around the corner, blowing back her skirts and twitching at the fringes of her shawl.

"Battle?" she said sharply. "And killing? Oh, Augusta!"

"Oh, dear, I didn't mean that," Augusta cried, flushing. "I meant—well, remember how thrilling it was when we heard about the *Ranger* taking prizes and capturing the *Drake,* and all that? That's all I mean, Priscilla."

"I know, Augusta. I'm sorry I snapped at you. Everyone snaps these days. Did you hear about Caroline's husband? He is not expected to live, they say, even though she's been there nursing him day and night."

"Well, at least they were able to be married," Augusta said so wistfully that Priscilla managed to restrain herself from snapping again. Augusta, she thought, truly had no one. Her only real friend had been Helen, and now Helen and her husband were in New Hampshire visiting with his family for several weeks. He would rejoin his regiment, Priscilla had been told. Then Helen would come back to her mother's small house in Portsmouth again, looking older, sadder, more subdued than ever. As she left Augusta and hurried on toward Atkinsons' with a message from her mother, Priscilla wondered if it was indeed better to have someone to worry so about, or if one was as well off having, like Augusta Peirce, no one at all. Priscilla remembered Helen's dark and vital good looks as she

stood in front of the fireplace on that first occasion, her
arm along the mantelpiece and her red dress glowing. The
last time she had seen her, Helen's face was gray and worn,
the sparkle in her dark eyes gone, the full mouth stiff and
still. What a horrible time to live in, she thought resentfully. But maybe things will be better now that March is
gone. Even the rains of April are an improvement over
gusty, bleak old March, although so far the wind does not
seem to know April is here, but huffs and puffs and freezes
a body to death. And, suddenly lonely, she decided to stop
in at Dorothy's. Company was wanted, and a sympathetic
ear.

That afternoon Dorothy and Priscilla made a pact to
see each other more frequently.

"We must ask Augusta and Mary and Helen, when she
comes back, and Anna too, I suppose, to take tea with us
once a week, if we can," Dorothy suggested. "We must
see people, Pris. It's the winter, I suppose. Colonel James
says he can't remember a longer one, with more snow.
Colonel James said another year like this one and he would
close up the place and go and work with Uncle Elijah at
Langdon's. But that part is over with, and we can get
about more."

The end of the winter and their determination to see
their friends more often made a great difference in their
lives. Helen returned, her husband gone once more, and as
usual her presence reminded them all of the flag, the slender thread that tied the Quilting Party together. They
waited anxiously, individually and in their "meetings," as
Helen liked to call them, although the get-togethers were
purely social now and centered around the drinking of tea
made from whatever usable bark or root happened to be
on hand.

Outwardly, Priscilla and the others behaved as usual.

They worked hard at home, They knitted and sewed for soldiers and sailors when they could find materials to work on. They took care of children, substituting in homes when mothers left for brief sojourns with fighting husbands, or when tragedy fell over a household. They ripped up garments and turned them inside out to make them appear less faded and worn. They kept busy from morning until night and fell into sleep that was threaded through with uneasy dreams. The news was sometimes good and sometimes bad, but no end to the war was in sight.

Finally, in July, they learned that the *Bonhomme Richard* had at last been fitted out to the Captain's satisfaction and had sailed. Priscilla had a long letter from Mark about it. "We are about three hundred and seventy-five, but only fifty or so, including the officers, are American. That seems odd, does it not? It does to me, I must own. Walking about our decks is like taking a trip around the world, you might say, as one hears French and Portuguese and of course the odd English speech, a sort of slang it is, of the British prisoners of war. There are Swedes too, and Norwegians, Swiss, Irish, Italians, and even a couple of East Indians. You see, we have quite a squadron, thanks, I am told, to the Marquis de Lafayette, who is an old friend of the Captain and most influential at Court. We are the *Alliance, Pallas, Vengeance* and *Cerf*—and of course ourselves, the fine *Bonhomme Richard.*

"We sailed from L'Orient on June 19, had trouble straightaway and back to port with us. Six weeks more of waiting—I did not write to you in all that time, Priscilla, because they were black weeks for me. I could not think somehow just what I was doing there, it so foreign and me accomplishing nothing at all but hanging about hating the place, although once I had liked it well enough. I could not picture where I should be if I were elsewhere either, and it was that that disturbed me the most, I suppose. At home, yes, but who and what would I be there? Mark Jaffrey, looking for odd jobs again? Would Mr. Livermore take me back to study, or would he tell me that my mind has rusted away and is not worth bothering with now? He might, you know.

"Well, enough of that. Tomorrow we will be off again, looking for action. And now we think we will find plenty of that."

He ended the letter so abruptly that Priscilla wondered if he hadn't found action already. She began to worry about him more than she ever had before. Then she realized that if he had indeed found "action," and at the very moment when he stopped writing the letter, it was all over now. It didn't prevent the worrying, but she found that at least she could stop imagining dreadful sea battles and could concentrate on waiting for a frigate or packet to stop in the harbor with mail and news.

"It's the waiting!" she wailed to Dorothy. "Just not knowing. It takes so long to hear anything."

"Better than having it happen where you can sit on a rooftop and watch," Dorothy said philosophically. "This way you don't *know* how bad it is, Pris, and you can keep telling yourself your imagination is too vivid."

"Well, it is, sometimes," Priscilla said sadly. "Oh, dear, here it is almost September, and we haven't heard another word."

Much later she learned that for forty days after the sailing from Isle de Groix early in August, they found little of that action, but when it came at last, it kept them all busy. On September 23 there had been action aplenty when the *Bonhomme Richard* fought the British frigate *Serapis*.

The *Gazette* was full of it, of course, and letters brought home by fast merchantmen were devoured and passed from hand to hand. What mattered at first was the great victory of the *Bonhomme Richard.* Then as later reports of the sea fight rolled in, people counted up the frightful cost in lives. Through it all the figure of Commodore Paul Jones stood out clearly in every word picture. His stirring words, when asked by the captain of the *Serapis* if he had struck his colors, echoed through the quiet streets of Portsmouth, passing from mouth to ear, "I have not yet begun to fight!"

Most dramatic and blood-chilling of all was the news that at the last minute, and apparently in the nick of time, the living and the many wounded had been transferred to the captured *Serapis.* The stricken *Bonhomme Richard,* although the victor, had sunk in forty fathoms of water.

Not even the Quilting Party thought of their flag. Everyone in Portsmouth, even the women and the many men who had never been to sea and who certainly had never been engaged in battle, could visualize some of the action through the descriptions sent home by the men aboard the *Richard* that day. Everyone could picture the last moment of the ship, sinking after two nights and a day of valiant efforts by the survivors to save her. Fires were put out. Attempts were made to stop leaks. Pumps were worked at full speed. But on the evening of the twenty-fourth of September, a day and a half after the battle, John Paul Jones agreed that his ship was past saving. The next morning the Commodore and his men watched as the *Bonhomme Richard* sank, bow first, into the waters of the North Sea.

All this time, reports stated, Surgeon Brooke and his mates had been working feverishly trying to save the wounded, but the dead had been sent to the bottom with the ship. Priscilla and Betsy couldn't even speak of it. They stared wordlessly at each other with eyes dark and wide with worry and fear. Mark *must* be wounded, Priscilla said to herself, or he would have written to her. He always had written so cheerfully about what had happened that one would think him a spectator at the action, invisible and therefore safe. Or had he been one of those who had gone to the depths of the ocean on the *Richard*? How could she bear it? How could she go about her everyday life and appear natural and unconcerned? For the first time Priscilla realized what had happened to the others, to Helen and Caroline and to all the women she knew who had husbands or sweethearts on a fighting front or at sea.

"Mark is nothing to me really," she said to Dorothy, twisting her hands together nervously in a way that was new to her, "and yet I am so—frightened, Dorothy."

"Are you sure he is nothing to you, Pris?" Dorothy spoke with a quiet gravity as new as Priscilla's taut gestures. "Perhaps he has meant more to you than you think, all this time."

Priscilla nodded. "Yes, I suppose so. Just having all those letters from him, and knowing that I was the only one he wrote to. Or at least I suppose I'm the only one. Anyway, I just began to realize lately that I looked forward to his letters so and read them over and over as though he were —well, Daniel Wendell and I were Betsy. But I guess it's just because of the war and I sort of dramatize things. At least, that's what Mother said to me one day when I was in a mood about it."

"Perhaps she thought you were mooning over the Captain," Dorothy suggested shrewdly. "Well, I won't go so far as poor Augusta and tell you it's better to be left than never to have loved, but I do think it's good to have someone to—to worry over, at least."

"I don't!" Priscilla could hardly bear the mental pictures of Mark falling wounded to a deck or—or worse.

"It isn't right just to—to float," Dorothy commented sadly. "Although—well, of course I see your point of view. I guess I'm wrong, and I won't say it again. But do cheer up, Pris. You don't *know* anything's wrong—you just suspect it, you know. Don't borrow trouble, that's what Aunt Elizabeth is always telling me. It's good advice."

"Yes, it is," Priscilla stood up briskly. "Now I'll go home and try to smile, and I'll take one look at Betsy's long face and—I'll be just as gloomy as I was when I came here. But thank you anyway, Dorothy. You tried!"

Chapter 13

THE SEVENTH STAR

IT WAS THE END of October, and Priscilla was struck by the fact that it had been two whole years since the Quilting Party had met at Stoodley's Tavern and sewed on the Captain's flag. Two whole years! Sometimes it seemed a lifetime. At other times she couldn't believe that in a few days it would be the second anniversary of the *Ranger's* sailing from the harbor with their flag fluttering bravely in the bright November sun.

Still there had been no word from Mark, nor any about him. Since the fast ships had delivered the first accounts of the battle, no one had received further news. Few ships sailed in and out of the river's mouth anyway. They all seemed to be engaged elsewhere.

November moved in, a continuation of October with unexpectedly warm weather and bright sun-filled days, and the people of Portsmouth enjoyed a false sense of security. The weather was deceptive. It was easy to forget that soon snow would fly and salt hay should be piled up against foundations to keep the houses warm, that woodsheds must be filled to supply hungry fireplaces. Preparations for winter were put off day to day, while the weather held, because people liked to meet and talk and rest a little, while they could.

It had been more than six weeks since the battle that ended in the sinking of the *Bonhomme Richard.* There had been time to hear more about it, about the dead and wounded, but Priscilla along with the others found herself clinging to this period of waiting, willing it to turn to hope instead of despair.

"Evil news rides post," Dorothy insisted frequently, quoting Colonel James, and although Priscilla got tired of hearing the words, she took comfort from them just the same.

The third week in November saw the first change in the weather. The skies turned gray, and the sea was black and forbidding. Chill air swept eastward from the White Mountains, and people looking anxiously at the sky said, "It will snow soon, by the look of it."

At once there was a flurry of activity as the people of Portsmouth hurried to their kitchens and barns and quickly began belated preparations for winter. Priscilla and Betsy were sent outside by their mother to help Benjamin, the old man who did what little work they could have done around the garden and outside the house. Much against their will, they found themselves stacking against the base of the house the salt hay brought up from the marshes to the south.

"What has Benjamin been doing all these weeks?" Betsy asked angrily. "Anyone would think we were farm girls, for heaven's sake. Look at my hands, all blisters. I never used a pitchfork in my life!"

"Perhaps it's time you did." Priscilla didn't enjoy the task any more than her sister did, but the physical action seemed to soothe something in her. "Poor old Benjamin, he has other houses than ours to look after now, with every-one away at the war, even most of the servants. Look over there."

Betsy leaned on the handle of her pitchfork and unwill-ingly looked where Priscilla was pointing. Old Mrs. Whip-ple and the fourteen-year-old niece, who was her ward, were doing their best to push a mound of marsh grass against their own house, but they were working with brooms.

"Benjamin," called Priscilla, "run over and help Mrs. Whipple. We can finish up here."

"Oh, Priscilla, we'll never get done," Betsy wailed.

"Sooner than she will—she's an old lady. And the girl has arms like sticks. Come on, you won't finish if you don't work, you know."

Even Priscilla was glad when the task was completed. Her hands ached from holding the hoe, and her palms were raw and blistered. Her back ached too, and she thought she would never be able to stand up straight again. The air was bitter now, and the wind pushed its sharp edges through her clothes into her body.

"I can't eat supper. I can't do anything," she moaned to Betsy, who was letting tears of exhaustion roll down her face. "Mother can't ask us to—to so much as move, after this afternoon's work."

Betsy nodded and rubbed at her tears, leaving black streaks on her face. Wearily they entered the house, paus-ing only to warm themselves at the fire in the dining room. Early as it was, the table was set for supper and the fire had been lighted, but no one was about.

"I'd go to bed even if it is the middle of the afternoon, but I don't think I can climb all the way upstairs," Betsy moaned. "All those steps. Oh, Pris, I *ache* so."

"I—" Priscilla began. Suddenly there was a pounding at the kitchen door that rattled the china in the cupboards and made the teacups dance on their saucers. The sisters stared at each other. An alarm? A fire? An attack of some kind? What could it be?

For an instant they were frozen where they were, but Priscilla recovered first and rushed out through the pantry to the kitchen. It was, of all people, she thought dazedly, Josiah Whipple who stood there. She had seen Josiah two or three times from a distance, but never up close since the fateful evening in Sheafe's warehouse. The story of the "guests from Salem" had finally grown to include him, and it developed that Josiah had been at the warehouse in the hope of catching the culprits himself. Priscilla judged that he would have no great love for her for spoiling his act of patriotism, so she had kept her distance. But now here he was in the doorway of her own kitchen, beaming at her across the room.

"It's Miss Priscilla I have come for," he exclaimed, waving Caddie aside. Caddie, for all her great bulk, professed to be timid and afraid, but now she advanced on the big youth as though she intended to protect the others. "There is a friend of yours, Miss Priscilla," Josiah went on, ignoring Caddie and the others, "who will be glad of the sight of you."

"But—"

"The brig *Fannie* just came into harbor," Josiah said, grinning widely. "She has come all the way from Holland, she has, and aboard her there are wounded from the *Richard*. Jeremy Cleaves, he sailed out to her as she came into the river's mouth, and he talked to some of the men. There is Mark Jaffrey aboard, Miss Priscilla, who was wounded, they tell me, but he says as how he would like to see you, and so I—"

"Mark!" Priscilla shrieked. "Oh, my cloak. Where is my bonnet? No matter, this shawl will do. Oh, dear, I am a mess—is my face as dirty as Betsy's? Quick, Caddie, give me that cloth there. Molly, do you have your comb in your pocket? Oh, never mind, what does it matter how I look? I will go—"

"Priscilla Purcell, you will wash your face and make yourself presentable before you go anywhere. Do you understand me?"

"But, Mother Mark—"

"I heard what was said. But not even a man who is ending a long voyage across the sea would wish to be welcomed by a face such as yours. Quick, Elizabeth, get a clean kerchief for her, and bring down the brush."

Betsy scrambled up the stairs and was down again in an instant. "What happened to all that fatigue you were complaining of?" she asked impishly.

"For that matter, what happened to yours?" Priscilla retorted. She caught a look of envy on Betsy's face and hugged her quickly. "I'm sorry, Betsy. Maybe Daniel is there too. Come with me."

"No," Betsy shook her head. "If he is not, it will be that much the worse. Has the ship tied up yet, Josiah?"

Josiah shook his straw-colored head over the cup of steaming soup Caddie had just handed him.

"No, Miss Elizabeth. She was at harbor's mouth when I left, and I came fast as I could run. We will be there afore she docks, you may be sure of that. If," he added, "too much primping isn't done meantime."

"I'm ready," Priscilla said evenly. "But finish your soup, Josiah."

He drained the cup in a gulp, and she wondered if he had scalded himself, but he only smiled broadly at Caddie as he handed back the cup. "I needed that, it was powerful good and mighty hot and comforting. Well, Miss Priscilla?"

"Bring Mark back here with you," Mrs. Purcell called after Priscilla. "If he is able, I mean, of course. We will find a bed for him either here or next door, and of course we can give him food. Do not run like a wild Indian, Priscilla, but remember that you are a Purcell and a lady. And Josiah, we thank you for coming to us, and for walking Priscilla back."

"There is no need to run, ma'am," Josiah said as soon as they were outside. "If you run, you will only have a long wait in the cold. I promise you we will get there before the *Fannie,* if you will suit your steps to mine."

Reluctantly, Priscilla fell into step with him. Because she must stop her mind from whirling so around a center that was Mark Jaffrey, she said, "I haven't seen you, Josiah, to tell you I'm sorry I—I was so stupid about the warehouse."

"No matter," he said cheerfully. "They was scared off, is the point of it all anyway."

"But I sort of came along and—and took the glory."

"What glory? I didn't want no glory, nor did you, I reckon. No, we wanted to put them fellas to rout, and that we did. Better if we had caught them maybe, and clapped them into jail if we could of found a right reason, but at least we rid ourselves of them. I never did know how you caught on to them though, Miss Priscilla."

"Oh, Josiah, stop calling me miss, for heaven's sake," she said with more anger than she felt. "Well, if you really must know, I didn't catch on to them, I thought it was you."

"Me! Oh, miss—I mean, why ever did you think it was me?"

"Well, I saw you there twice, and I didn't know if you had any right to be there, so I thought I'd set a trap and catch you somehow." She wouldn't tell him how she had felt about the new coach!

"But him, that pretty-face, how did you get him then?"

"I asked Dorothy Hall to help me, and she brought him along. He was her—friend, you see, and he was staying at Stoodley's, where she lives. And I guess he thought we'd found out about him, and so he—left."

Josiah threw back his tousled head and laughed heartily

"I never did," he said with amusement. "Set a trap for me and caught the right one by mistake! I don't blame you for thinking bad of me. Mr. Woodbury Langdon, he said afterward to me that I took a chance to be there like that, because who in town knew me or where my loyalty should be. But it come out right, for because of it all Mr. Woodbury Langdon, he gave me a job, and now Mr. John Langdon says will I come work in his shipyard, but I said no, because I aim to get into the navy. I've just been waiting for my father to settle down. He happen to make a packet of money on that privateer he shipped on, and will now catch him a new wife, to live in the house he bought. My mother died when I was small, you see."

Priscilla looked at him curiously. How little we know about the people around us, she thought. She was trying to phrase a polite remark about his father's happiness when Josiah pointed a big forefinger and said, "There, miss. There's the *Fannie*. Now we may hurry a bit, if you like."

Sailors on the frigate were just then tossing a rope to the wharf. Josiah and Priscilla reached her side before she was made fast. Priscilla searched the faces at the rail, looking for only one and not really seeing the others. The gangplank was thrown down, and slowly the men came off the ship, some silently, some waving and shouting. Priscilla sensed rather than saw a vast crowd behind her. People had appeared from nowhere and were thronging to the wharf as news of the arrival spread by magic over the town.

Finally she saw Mark. He was walking with difficulty, one arm over the shoulders of another man who had his arm in a sling. As he reached the top of the sloping gangplank he looked around. Almost at once his eyes met hers. In a quick rough gesture, he flung aside the man who had been supporting him, raised his chin high, and walked steadily down the incline.

Priscilla was quickly in his arms. She could smell the sea in his warm jacket, and smoke from the cookstove, and salt fish, and tar—and it smelled wonderful to her. His arms were tight around her, and his cheek rested on the scarf wound round her head.

"Priscilla," he murmured. "You are here. I am so glad to see you."

She looked up with tears in her eyes. "*You* are here," she replied. "That is what is so wonderful. Oh, Mark. But you're hurt, and you shouldn't be standing like this. You are coming home with me, my mother insists."

Before he could protest, Josiah had reached Priscilla's side. "Give me your bundle," he said. "And here, lean on me. Stavers has sent the stage here, you know, to take some of you chaps home. You are in the first load, so hurry, because the sooner you fellas get where you're bound the sooner the stage can come back for the others. So don't argue, but—but come. Come along, Miss Priscilla." They had Mark in the stage before he knew it.

"I'll see you at home, Mark," Priscilla cried, noticing with a pang how white and tired he looked, now that he was sitting in the chaise, crowded with four others on the seat meant to hold three. She waved cheerfully once more and started off at a run with Josiah beside her. He was swinging Mark's canvas bag as though it were a toy as they hurried through the darkening streets.

"Thank you, Josiah," she said, her eyes brimming with tears as they reached her house. "Will you come in? Caddie will give you supper."

"No, ma'am, thank you. There is others as could use some help tonight. Some of the men will want carrying, I judge. Your Mark is lucky." He looked down into her face. "In more ways than one," he added solemnly. Then he handed her the bag and disappeared into the dusk.

"Mark will have the Captain's old room, or rather the dressing room," Mrs. Purcell said as soon as Priscilla walked into the house. "Mr. Chauncey has agreed to give up the small room for a night or two, until we can make other arrangements, and Jerusha has made up a bed in there. You and Mark can have your supper in the counting room. I'm sorry, Priscilla, but that is the only space we have. The dining room is, of course, occupied, and I have, somewhat against my will, I own, told Mr. Mason he can have his Sons of Liberty committee meeting in the parlor."

Priscilla raised her eyebrows. Mrs. Purcell had steadfastly refused to have anything even vaguely political take place in her home. Since she had no man to defend her, she said, she did not want her house and seven daughters a target for any dissatisfied people at any time.

"The counting room will be perfect," Priscilla said. "I will carry in the food. Caddie and the others must be very busy."

"Betsy could do it," Mrs. Purcell said, "but I think that would be too—too—well, you know. Nothing of Daniel?"

"I didn't have a chance to ask Mark," Priscilla said. "But I will later."

It was some time before Mark was delivered to the door, and it took several minutes for him to walk up the garden, climb the steps, and enter the house. Mrs. Purcell made him welcome at once. Assured that he was well enough to eat supper and to sit and talk to Priscilla for a while, she showed him into the counting room. Priscilla brought them bread hot from the oven and bowls of Caddie's steaming soup. He ate hungrily at first, and then stopped.

"I have had nothing really *good* to eat for weeks and weeks and weeks," he confessed. "And now that I have—and it is so good—I can't seem to eat it. Too much all at once, I suppose. Getting here, and finding you waiting for me, and having your mother ask me to stay here . . . You know, I couldn't think where I could go, who would take me in! No, it is too much, truly, Pris. Do you understand?"

She nodded gravely. "Mark, can you tell me what happened? Or would you rather not talk about it?"

"You had my note? That I was wounded, but not seriously, and would probably soon be home?"

She shook her head. "And I was so worried."

"I was afraid that would happen," he admitted. "Things were in such a state, after the battle, and we were none of us sure that we could trust the people who were supposed to see that letters reached home. Did none of them get here?"

"All but yours! And—Daniel's. What of Daniel, Mark, do you know?"

"Why, yes, he was wounded very slightly, even less than I. He went back on duty immediately and is now with the Commodore in Amsterdam."

"Do you mind if I run and tell Betsy? I'll be right back."

Priscilla hurried to the kitchen and blurted out her news. Betsy, who was helping the girls to serve, promptly burst into tears and ran up the stairs.

"No matter, Miss Priscilla," Molly said cheerfully, "Jushy and me, we'll manage. Go on back to your young man."

Priscilla went back quickly. "Now," she said.

"I was wounded," Mark told her, "by one of our own ships. Yes, it's true. There was a Frenchman in charge of one of them, a madman by the way he acted, and he hated the Commodore. Well, I won't go into it, but he maneuvered athwart our bows and fired some shots at us. By luck one of them struck me just below the knee." He looked pensively into the fire, with his bad leg on a cushion placed on a chair in front of him. "Fortune of war, for sure. To be hit by one's own ships! It seemed to be bad at first, and it was thought I would lose my leg. But one of Surgeon Brooke's men decided it could be saved. He worked over me as long as he could, and I am as good as new. Or I will be, when I have had a little rest."

Then he turned to her and said, "Do you want to hear about it, Pris? The bad part? Or no?"

"Yes, I do," she said quietly. "All of it, Mark. I want to know everything."

"Well, the only people left on the *Richard* after that bloody battle were our own dead. They had got the rest of us off onto the *Serapis*, you see. When the Commodore saw there was no saving our ship, he had to let it go, and he gave it to our dead for a coffin."

Priscilla shivered, and Mark put his hand over hers gently. "It was best that way. Truly. Even though I could scarce stand with my wound, I dragged myself over to the rail to watch. She rolled slowly, the gundeck was awash, and she settled slowly by the head and sank. The last thing we saw, Priscilla, was your flag. He had left it there, he said, to honor the dead on the decks, who had given their lives to keep it flying."

"So that's what happened to it," Priscilla breathed. "We wondered. No one told us—isn't that strange?"

"I hope you don't mind, Pris, but it was right. It was right that he did what he did, I mean, instead of saving the flag and taking it along. It gave the dead glory to take with them, you see. That flag, so important to them and to us all, it was the greatest tribute he could give them at that moment. Do you mind?"

"Oh, of course not. As you say, it was so—so right."

"Yes," he agreed gravely. "I'm glad you feel that way. I hope the others do. He had meant to bring it back here, you see, to you girls who had made it. He told me so once. 'Untarnished into the fair hands which gave it.' Those were his words, I think. He even said, with that twinkle he shows now and then—not often, I must say!—'I wonder how the young ladies will divide it up among them! Perhaps it will be cut into bits.' But he was teasing, of course. Oh, funny thing, and I don't quite understand it myself, but I think perhaps the Commodore gave me a message for you."

"F-for me?" About the flag, she thought. He did think of me when he saw it!

"We were on deck one night—this was months ago, when we first sailed on the *Richard*. It just happened I was beside him, and no one else close by. He looked at me, and then at the flag, and he said, 'We are far from your Portsmouth, are we not? You and I and our flag. One day you will go back, and you must tell the young ladies how proudly their flag has been carried, all this time. And tell her particularly, Jaffrey. You will remember to do that?' "

Mark shifted in his chair and looked at her, his brown eyes bright and wide. "But how he knew that you and I—"

Priscilla patted his hand. The Captain knew—he had known long before she had herself, for that matter. Perhaps he had even known, or suspected, how she felt about *him*, and had in effect thus turned her over to Mark, forever.

"Strange," Mark went on, "I had forgotten all about that moment. So much happened later. But about the flag, he knew you honored it, as he did. Yet he let it go with the men who had fought for it so bravely. 'Unconquered and unstricken'—he said that of the flag. 'Unconquered and unstricken.' And now it is flying at the bottom of the sea over what is, as far as I know, the only ship that ever sank in victory."

Mark was silent, staring moodily into the fire. While she waited for him to speak again, Priscilla marveled at many things—at her easy acceptance of Mark's presence in the little counting room, of Mark himself, and most strange, of a relationship that was new and that existed without having been put into words. Now she understood about Mary Langdon and Peter Wendell—these things budded and bloomed beneath the surface and were suddenly and undeniably there, full-grown. Finally Mark turned and smiled at Priscilla, tightening his fingers on her hand.

"Pris, that part about dividing the flag up among you . . . I want to tell you something about that, if you promise not to laugh."

"Oh, Mark, of course I won't."

"You know, every time I looked at it—when I was not busy trying to save my life or take someone else's, that is— I thought of you. And I had an idea in my mind, a foolish one, I suppose, but each time I looked at it I had this notion that I was looking at the stitches you had taken, that I could see the very part of the flag that you made yourself."

"Which part did you pick, Mark?"

"A star," he said. "Especially during the night watch, when the sky was sometimes black as ink and the sea too, I would imagine the flag flying up there and one special star seemed to shine brighter than the rest."

"Which one?"

"Well," he said sheepishly, "looking at the circle of them, you see, if you choose this one here as the first and start to count round the circle like a clock face, it would be this one here." He checked off imaginary stars on the arm of the chair with his forefinger. "Here. One—two—three—four—five—six—seven. This one, you see, the seventh star. Seven has always been my lucky number."

Priscilla sat and stared at him for a moment. Then she put her free hand over Mark's and said, "But I did make that one. It was mine. The seventh star. And it was special, just as you say, to me too. The seventh star. I can't believe it."

"I can. I believe in things like that. At least, I do now. And I'll tell you something, Priscilla Purcell. It was that star that kept me alive, when I was out of my head with fever and pain. It kept me alive, and it brought me home again. I believe that with all my heart. Brought me home to you. Now I want to know something: Do you believe it too?"

"Yes, Mark," she said steadily, and she leaned close to him and kissed him gently. Although she had never kissed a young man before, nor been kissed by one, it seemed the most natural action in the world. "Yes, Mark, I do. With all my heart."

Notes from the Author

Priscilla Purcell, two of her sisters, and the descriptions and personalities of the other members of the Purcell family are pure invention. The basic facts, involving Sarah Wentworth Purcell, widow of Gregory, and of the "genteel boardinghouse" where John Paul Jones lived while he was in Portsmouth, are true. The house, now known as the John Paul Jones house and headquarters of the Portsmouth Historical Society, still stands.

Incomplete and contradictory accounts credit the Purcells with twelve children. In general they agree that of the twelve, seven—all girls—were alive when Captain Gregory died in 1776 at the age of forty-two after seventeen years of marriage. Known children appear to be: Gregory (one source says he died in 1788 at the age of eighteen, which doesn't jibe with the "seven daughters" claim); Mary, born in 1767; Sarah, 1769; Margaret (no date, but she had a daughter who married in 1823); and Susan, 1777. To this somewhat fragmentary record I have boldly added my fictitious Elizabeth, Priscilla, and Hannah.

Since I invented Priscilla to begin with, I cheerfully added her, as well as her sister Betsy, to the Quilting Party. Of this group Helen Seavey, Mary Langdon, Augusta Peirce, Dorothy Hall, and Caroline Chandler appear to have been real. The Purcell sisters and Anna Hilton are all mine. Dorothy Hall was indeed the niece of Elijah Hall, who sailed as lieutenant on the *Ranger* and whose wife was the daughter of Colonel James Stoodley, owner of Stoodley's Tavern. This tavern, which has been moved to become part of the enormously interesting and valuable Strawbery Banke restoration in Portsmouth, has been used for the setting of the historic quilting party.

The dates of the quilting party and of the presentation of the flag are far from clear. One source says that July 4, 1777, the first anniversary of the signing of the Declaration of Independence, was the day when John Paul Jones made a special trip from Boston to receive his gift. Others feel the presentation was made just before the *Ranger* sailed. This seems more logical, so I have arbitrarily adopted October 29 as the date for *my* quilting party, and October 31 as the day the flag was given to the Captain.

The flag and its subsequent history are a matter of record, and add a shining footnote to a page in the history of our country. Betsy's Daniel Wendell is real—although he was to die at sea in 1780, I'm afraid—but Mark Jaffrey, Josiah Whipple, Samuel Otis, and all of the boarders at Purcells' (except John Paul Jones, of course) are fictitious. For the most part I borrowed Portsmouth names for my characters. Local geography of the day is taken from the map prepared by Dorothy Vaughan and Harold G. Rundlett, in 1930, and copyrighted by H. G. Rundlett, and from the *Official Guidebook* of Strawbery Banke.

I am indebted and most grateful to Dr. Dorothy M. Vaughan, head librarian of the extremely useful Portsmouth Public Library, for unstinting help and advice. Miss Vaughan is also a historian of note and the prime mover in the historical restoration project called Strawbery Banke, which is becoming an important national shrine. Without Miss Vaughan's unending fund of knowledge and generous cooperation, this book could not exist—but if there are unwitting errors to be found on its pages, she is in no way to blame.

Bibliography

Brewster, Charles W., *Rambles About Portsmouth*. Portsmouth: published by Lewis W. Brewster, 1873.

Buell, Augustus C., *Paul Jones, Founder of the American Navy*. New York: Charles Scribner's Sons, 1901.

Chamberlain, Samuel, *Portsmouth, New Hampshire*. New York: Hastings House, 1940.

Kappel, Philip, *New England Gallery*. Boston: Little, Brown and Company, 1966.

Morison, Samuel Eliot, *John Paul Jones*. Boston: Little, Brown and Company, 1959.

New Hampshire, Federal Writer's Project. Boston: Houghton Mifflin Company, 1938.

Upton, Richard Francis, *Revolutionary New Hampshire*. Hanover: Dartmouth College Publications, 1936.

Wentworth, John, *The Wentworth Genealogy*, Vol. I. Boston: Little, Brown and Company, 1878.

Biography of Marjory Hall

Marjory Hall has been writing something most of her life—majoring in English composition at Wellesley and writing editorial pages and booklets for the *Ladies' Home Journal*, advertising copy, a scattering of stories and articles taking on whatever writing assignment has come along. The *Journal* job was in the Sub-Deb Department, and from that stems her interest in teen-age girls. After writing for them, she ran a department store promotion for the *Journal*, traveling around the country and visiting the stores where teen-agers congregated to see fashion and other shows, until a few thousand girls in the country were calling her Midge.

Because of the several years' experience as teen-age adviser, she wrote for a couple of years a twice-a-week column called "Talking to Teens" for the late *Boston Transcript*, and later turned to books of career fiction for girls and historical novels. For several years she has been travel and resort editor for *Yankee Magazine*.

After many years in advertising as a copywriter and executive, she retired to become a free-lance writer and advertising consultant. When she is not traveling around the country on business, she is traveling outside it for pleasure. Her husband is a lawyer, and they live in a modern glass-fronted house on the edge of the ocean, which during the summer months they seem to be on when they're not in. Most of her life has been lived in New England, with a few years here and there spent in Philadelphia and New York.

М